T0165265

Steeled with a Kiss

VERONICA NEILL

iUniverse, Inc.
Bloomington

Steeled with a Kiss

This is a work of fiction. All of the characters, names, incidents, organizations, and dialogue in this novel are either the products of the author's imagination or are used fictitiously.

iUniverse books may be ordered through booksellers or by contacting:

iUniverse
1663 Liberty Drive
Bloomington, IN 47403
www.iuniverse.com
1-800-Authors (1-800-288-4677)

ISBN: 978-1-4502-5915-6 (sc)
ISBN: 978-1-4502-5916-3 (ebook)
ISBN: 978-1-4502-5917-0 (dj)

Library of Congress Control Number: 2010915838

Printed in the United States of America

iUniverse rev. date: 4/7/2011

For Barbara:

Plus qu'hier, moins que demain.

Lenny didn't know what to do with the gun. He had swiped it from Gary two days ago, but he had lost the satisfaction in thwarting his friend's suicide. Now there was something else. Nothing prepared him to understand the possession of a firearm.

Gary thought ***his*** *life sucked in a way that ending it would provide the only option. Lenny felt his own life was even more pathetic. Here he sat, an accidental musician, lucky enough in timing and circumstance to be a part of an ensemble of a talented and successful group. He feared that the truth would surface—he was a fraud—and he would be cast out. That he was marrying a woman that he loved as a friend but not well enough to be a lover only exposed his forgery of a life. Gary was right on that account—Lenny didn't deserve Penny. And he hated it that Gary was right.*

Lenny was torn. He could spiral into a foul mood that spun between personal culpability and moral obligation, or he could nurture the anger that would find its way to Gary. Neither provided a moral high road. But both options accommodated the solution he held in his hand.

Lenny stared at the gun, at the iPod dock that was stuck on "Folsom Prison Blues," at the mirror that showed his own enamored fascination with the gun, then the iPod. He didn't remember turning on the Cash song, or hitting the replay that looped Cash's song over and over. Or was he looking for a blueprint?

"Enough,*" he said aloud, the first word he spoke that day. Taking the gun, he left the room.*

Prologue

Fiona Clarke sensed it was coming. The moment her head lifted from the pillow that morning, she had had an itchy feeling on the roof of her mouth. The itch was the sign. All she could do now was to wait. It would come sooner than later; she already knew that. She didn't even bother rubbing the itch with her tongue. She had learned quickly that it wasn't a real itch. It wouldn't do any good anyway.

The itch would stay until she *knew.*

Even at her present age of nine, Fiona recognized the need to classify this condition. She had in fact condensed her knowing into words, hoping to explain them someday, first to her mother, then her sister, who trailed her through Hancock Academy (Fiona was in the fourth grade, Angie in third). But as was true with the important things in life, the timing was always off, the setting wrong. And so Fiona sat with a growing list of facts she had compiled, big and small. From last year's knowing at breakfast that Angie would twist her ankle on the playground to the day that the man she and Angie secretly referred to as "The Hulk" proposed to their mother. Fiona had also known that their mother would accept The Hulk's proposal, and they were married within a few months.

She pulled on a pair of jeans and her favorite sweater, a ritual she had begun when she put two and two together. She had been wearing the sweater when her particular prescience gnawed itself into her awareness a year or so ago. Then the sweater was still baggy, before her present growing spurt. The sweater was now getting tight, and Fiona briefly wondered about the day it would no longer fit her. Would she grow out of this freaky talent too?

Fiona, staring at her white lacquered vanity mirror, resisted for a minute, a small rebellion that had little energy; then resolve overtook her. Closing her eyes, she started her mental inventory. Mother? Angie? No, neither one. Tony (a.k.a. The Hulk)? Wishful thinking, she mused, but not him either. Maybe someone at school—

Yes.

Okay. Fiona exhaled, relieved that it wasn't anyone in her family. Sometimes she did have good knowings about people, but Fiona had learned that it was best to wish the knowing away from anyone she really cared for. And school was just school, unless—

You know who, Fiona.

"No," she whispered, wanting to deny the voice.

But somehow she did know. Not all the details yet, but enough. Enough to know that when the final bell dismissed her from school, she would be seeing her favorite teacher for the last time.

* * * * * * * * * * *

"Fiona?" Dr. Marc Hawthorne addressed her as the others rushed out of the door.

Fiona looked around the room, surprised by what she saw. All the other students were in a hurry to leave. She hadn't even heard the bell but quickly gathered her things and rose from her desk.

Dr. Hawthorne knew that something was bothering his favorite student. Fiona's dyslexia, only barely discernible since Christmas, was much more pronounced. Even the essay on her spring break plans had been a problem for this young redhead. "So, Fiona, it sounds as if you're headed for a nice vacation." Dr. Hawthorne was gathering his own books and papers and stuffing them in his tan leather briefcase. Unlike Fiona's stepfather, who was a short, stocky man, Dr. Hawthorne was perhaps a few inches taller than her mother, which would put him just shy of six feet. He had almost delicate features that one first glance fooled many about his gender—student and teacher alike. Fiona felt comfortable with him. She was tall for her age, like her mother; she would be a giant among her peers even after puberty ended. Fiona was the tallest student in Dr. Hawthorne's class and had plenty of growing to do. Dr. Hawthorne was in his thirties, according to the 411 on the playground. Unfortunately for him, potential for a growth spurt was history.

Fiona realized that her teacher had asked a question and cleared her throat. "The Hulk—I mean, Tony—is taking us to Disney World." Fiona feigned excitement, but it flopped.

Dr. Hawthorne's hazel eyes opened widely; then he laughed. "The Hulk?"

Fiona smiled for the first time that day. "Yeah, but don't tell my mother I said that."

"Our secret," her teacher said, zipping his lips in a graceful arc of movement.

This is your chance.

"And you?" Fiona asked.

Her teacher shook his head. "Just staying here. Grading homework. A teacher's job is never done."

Dr. Hawthorne must have read something in her face; she saw his eyebrows indicate the question that followed. "Fiona, are you okay?"

"If I tell you something, will you promise not to—not to think I'm crazy or weird?" The question came out before Fiona could stop it.

"Fiona, I'd never think you are—"

"Fee-o-na!"her mother sang as she entered the room with her

usual dramatic flair. "Hurry up! You were supposed to meet us in the parking lot. Tony and Angie are in the car." Then she noticed Fiona's science teacher. "Oh, Dr. Hawthorne, I didn't see you." She barely altered her path, yet the air tensed with a subtle energy of attraction.

Fiona normally used all means necessary to steer her mother away from interaction with Dr. Hawthorne, as she knew her mother had developed a crush on him. Fiona suspected that some of her mother's fascination with Dr. Hawthore centered around his race and economic status, that he was an attractive black man with the extra benefits of intelligence and success on his side. Unfortunately for her mother, she had settled with low-hanging fruit and married Tony the Hulk.

She wished she had met her family in the parking lot as planned.

For once, Mrs. Clarke-Luminelli left him alone; she was that excited about going to Disney World. "Well, Fee, you're holding up your teacher as well as your family. Get a move on!"

Dr. Hawthorne opened his mouth to say something, but to Fiona's relief, he didn't. Fiona shrugged and grabbed her books. As she did, she dropped a small, folded paper. The note fluttered lazily to the floor.

Just as her teacher was about to mention that she had dropped something, Fiona caught his eye and shook her head slightly. "Good-bye, Dr. Hawthorne," she said, and then trailed her mother, who had barely disappeared around the door. She turned one last time. "You've been a great teacher," she said, then disappeared out the door.

* * * * * * * * * * *

Marc watched Fiona leave the room, momentarily distracted by his pupil's words. *Been a great teacher*? Children can be so unwittingly dramatic at this age, he mused as he gathered the briefcase, turned off the light, and closed the door.

Fiona's note of warning lay on the floor, unheeded.

One

A strong midnight wind swept Gary off Michigan Avenue and into the lobby of the Old Starlight Hotel. Dwarfed by the formidable Hancock Building and cradled by the glitterati of Chicago's Magnificent Mile, Old Starlight served as a point in contrast, a reminder of a time when luxury accommodations took on a smaller, yet more refined definition. Its petite facade opened to a series of intimate parlors where tête-à-têtes were absorbed by rich velvets and soothed by floral designs, unlike the typical glass block and rushing waterfalls of cavernous lobbies.

Even as he walked through the splendor of textured fabrics and antiques, Gary wasn't in much of a mind to admire his surroundings. Nor was he concerned about civil conversation. What he needed was to lose himself in the comfort of a scotch and the company of men. Here he could do both. For it was on this evening the diminutive hotel was host to the annual Blue Vista Ball. He hadn't been to this particular gay soiree before, but had vaguely recognized the name of the benefit when he saw it on the hotel's marquee. The rainbow flag displayed beneath the sign edged his memory along. Since he was already in the neighborhood, Gary could think of nothing better to distract him from his foul mood.

His friend Penny lived only a few blocks away. He had waited at her condo for more than an hour. She stood him up. It was the wrong night to stand him up.

Gary paid for his ticket at a table draped with hot-pink linen, then tried to tuck his frustration away as efficiently as his platinum card as he walked from the parlor into the ballroom.

"I probably look straight out of the Wild, Wild Fucking West," he muttered to no one in particular as he clopped across the dance floor with his cowboy boots and bolo tie. As he reached the bar, he ordered a drink and scanned the crowd.

The dance floor was far from crowded. Gary blamed it on the lateness of the hour and the bad choice of music. As much as people tried to resuscitate it, disco was dead. He wished that these folks would stop looking for its resurrection. As a result, all the small tables on the periphery held the most promise for distraction.

Scanning the occupants of both tuxes and sequined gowns, he caught the eye of an attractive blond who didn't seem too interested in table talk. *What the hell.* Gary raised his glass. Blondie smiled. They both continued to stare. *Maybe this evening wasn't a bust after all,* he mused as Blondie winked. Suddenly much less interested in the scotch than the company of men, Gary headed toward the door with an occasional glance behind him. Blondie followed.

* * * * * * * * * *

Blondie was not interested in the conversation at his table, precisely because he was the topic.

"Oh, snap out of it," Jules pleaded as his single friend stared across the room with sad eyes. "Haven't you mourned enough? D1 is gone. You've got to start checking out the other girls." When Jules said girls, he really meant boys.

Pete joined the attack. "You know he's right. You certainly make a lousy celibate. Look at you. You know what they say about 'all work and no play.' Jules says that you practically live in that office of yours. Go on vacation or something. Maybe the shopping's better out of town." They had previously discussed the lack of interesting bodies on the dance floor. Most were depressingly familiar faces. "Maybe you should come with me. Since Julie here won't go with me, I could use some company." Pete was leaving to visit his family in Boston.

"I'm here, aren't I?" Blondie replied, more tired of this conversation than usual. Rather than giving his best friends the airwaves as they redesigned his miserable life, he cut to the chase. "Just because you two have a good thing going doesn't mean it happens for everyone—"

He lost his thought as a man walked into the room with a purposeful stride. His hair was raven black and slightly longer than the current style, which only softened his precisely chiseled face. He looked vaguely familiar—as if Blondie had seen him before. Blondie kept his eye on Cowboy as he walked across the dance floor to the bar. He watched Cowboy order a drink and then lean against the counter with the indifference beautiful people seemed to possess. Even from a distance he could tell this one had a very fine ass.

Jules and Pete noticed no difference as they continued on with their amateur psychoanalysis. Well, almost no difference.

"Did you just wink?" Jules asked, shooting his glance across the floor.

"Just a business associate. I'll say good-bye on my way out," he said as he left the table, a halfhearted wave indicating his exit.

Pete looked at his lover. "Well, we had to do it. He needs to get bitched at by people who love him. He'll be okay," he said, patting his lover's hand.

Jules watched as their friend walked out the door, just seconds after a handsome brunette. "That old dog." Jules smirked.

"What?" asked Pete.

"God, I felt like I suddenly was transported back to my hometown church. Nothing like paying sixty-five bucks to get preached at. I could have watched a Billy Graham revival for free. And who was that fat guy at the end?"

The other comments were even less complimentary of the fat guy.

Penny groaned and quickly waved down her cab. "Just drive north," she said as a stream of loud music—were they playing "Just As I Am?"—blasted her into the backseat. "I'll tell you where to stop." She slammed the door, opened the door to free her purse, then slammed it shut again.

The cabdriver assessed his newest customer in the rearview mirror, a necessary habit honed after his first holdup and polished shiny from years of practice. A white woman in her thirties, probably mid-thirties, taller than the average woman, since she had to duck into the cab with deliberation as a tall person did. She wore black jeans, an untucked oversized white tux shirt, a bolo, and a red fringe jacket and boots. She had a lot of long, thick hair, shades ranging between dark blond and brown. Her eyes were dark, probably brown. He couldn't tell for sure. Overall, a nice-looking lady.

He figured she was a musician, though at least she hadn't been responsible for the noise being pumped out of that big church complex where he had picked her up. She had that performer type of attitude: self-absorbed. She also wore a lot of makeup.

He also knew that she would never remember a plain Joe like him. These types never did.

"Just north?" he asked.

"For now," she replied as she squirted hand cream on a tissue. "Would you turn on the light for a second?"

The overhead light went on. She scrubbed her face, consulting a hand mirror to assess the damage. She attempted to run a brush through her hair, which succeeded in making it bigger. "Never mind. You can turn it off now," she said.

He had picked her up on the north collar of Lincoln Park and now they were driving through Chicago's Lakeview neighborhood, a North Side district often referred to as Boys' Town. Many of the city's gay male population lived, worked, and shopped here. Though it was a Friday night, there were few people out.

"Where's everyone tonight?" Penny asked.

"Don't know. Maybe they were all at your concert, eh?"

Penny snickered. "Doubtful. I don't think this crowd would be too welcome at that little party."

They drove in silence down Broadway Avenue; then without consultation he turned onto Montrose Avenue. He didn't like driving through Uptown so close to midnight. He drove a few blocks, then asked her again, "Ma'am, do you have any idea where you would like to go?"

"Yeah. Turn on Ravenswood. Then, uh—"

"Just drive north," he finished.

They continued down Montrose until Ravenswood Avenue, then followed the small street north. The train tracks for one of the city's rail services jutted above them on their left. Old newspapers blew erratically against the embankment. The warm wind filled a plastic grocery bag like a helium balloon, floating it up to the tracks. A train came quickly, warning lights circling. The plastic bag had no chance as it collided with the ongoing train. The train continued on, disappearing down the dark tracks.

Ravenswood Avenue turned into a disappointing collection of small factories, loft conversions, new town houses, shuttered businesses, and road construction. They passed a gas station and convenience store at Foster Avenue.

"This is about as good as it gets," the driver said.

"We'll turn around at Peterson," she said. "There's a little restaurant down here. I haven't been there for a few months, but—" She stopped, wondering why she was explaining herself to a stranger.

"Restaurants close up pretty quick, especially off the beaten track like this," he commented. "And this late, well—" He figured he didn't need to finish his sentence either.

A few blocks later they reached their destination: half a dozen storefronts, containing an open restaurant and a bar huddled together for comfort on Balmoral Avenue. "Stop here." The lights from the restaurant winked out as if punctuating her sentence.

"Here? Are you sure?" The driver turned around and took a good long look. "I think the restaurant just closed, ma'am. And I don't think the bar is your kind of place."

"Oh yeah? Why not? Aren't women allowed?" Penny asked.

"Well, yeah, but—"

"How much do I owe you?" Penny cut him off as she handed him a twenty and got out. He looked at her, thinking that she might change her mind. She waved him on. He shrugged, then pulled away.

* * * * * * * * * * *

Just as Lenny hailed the cab, he jumped as someone tapped him on the shoulder. "Lenny, is that you?" a woman asked. "I haven't seen you for a long time. I'm glad you came out for the benefit."

"Uh, yeah," he said as he slid into the cab. "Great," he muttered. Old fucking home week.

The auburn-haired women didn't let him go that easily. "Is everything okay with you?" she asked. "I know you're engaged now. I was so surprised to hear about that."

"Well, Dale, I've changed a lot," he said, slamming the door.

"You certainly have," she replied to the closed cab door. She watched Lenny turn away from her, effectively cutting off further contact.

"Who's that, honey?" a man asked as he slid an arm around Dale.

"Lenny Blue," Dale Sentry said absently.

"The dude from 'Save the Chukkas'? The one on the Grammys?"

Dale nodded. "I have a feeling he's in way over his head."

* * * * * * * * * * *

Penny stood, unsure of her options. The door of the restaurant opened, and the owner slid out, locking the door. He saw Penny. "Good evening, love," he said with an accent that usually made Penny wonder whether she was in America or England. This time, however, it contained a bit of a chill. "Haven't seen you in quite a long time."

"Yeah," she replied to Clive. "With the band and everything, well, you know how it is. I see you're closing."

"It was a slow night. Thought I might as well pack it in. But I could make you a sandwich, if you'd like. Unless Lenny would somehow get jealous."

Suddenly her choice of location didn't seem so brilliant an idea. "No, don't be silly. And besides, I'm not really that hungry," she lied. Penny hadn't eaten since morning. "I'll just get a drink next door and be on my way."

"Want some company?" he asked.

She stood and seriously considered the proposition, because she knew that was exactly what it was. After all, wasn't that why she had come in the first place? "You know, I'd probably be lousy company for anyone tonight. But thanks for the offer."

"Suit yourself." He pulled her toward him; his kiss was hard, almost aggressive. "You know, it's not too late to admit to Lenny that the engagement is a mistake. It is a mistake, isn't it?"

Penny looked away. "Some people would have said the same thing about us."

He stepped back. "You didn't seem to think that a few weeks ago when you just happened to show up at my restaurant. Besides, I don't give a damn what others think." He stopped and looked at her. "Ah, but you do. Is that what this is about?" He held out his arms as if he just noticed the darkness of his skin color. "I'll be damned. I guess you like your boys a bit more on the pale side." He slowly disappeared down the quiet street.

"That's not what I meant!" The wind stole her words away. She was sure he didn't hear her. "Damn," she muttered, not completely sure if she believed her own assertion.

A gust of wind battered the flag hanging over the entrance of the bar. Two women stumbled out of the bar, so skunked that they were holding each other up. Penny decided that getting drunk off her ass wasn't a bad idea after all. She brushed the flag aside and entered. Inside, a dozen or so people sat around mismatched tables and sprawled on couches. After tripping on the flyers and freebie newspapers just inside the doorway, Penny made her way to the counter. "Martini. Dirty," Penny requested from the barkeep.

The place was almost completely populated with women, some who were as snookered as the ones she had passed on the way inside. Their inhibitions had been broken down so completely that they were holding hands and kissing—

Then it hit her. The women she had passed outside had not been drunk. They were merely being affectionate. Penny had happened into a lesbian bar.

Of course, the flag. The rainbow flag. It was hanging over the door like a big exclamation point. No wonder why the cabby hesitated to drop her off here. She noticed her drink was already empty. "Another, please." Penny watched the bartender. "How long have you been open?" she asked, then wondered if there was anything sexual about the question.

"Awhile. New in town?" The bartender set the second drink in front of her. Her expressive, handsome face with mocha eyes examined Penny. She had short, wavy hair with warm red tones that accentuated her brown skin.

"Well, I'm actually not from around here. I'm in town for a conference. From Iowa," Penny lied.

"Well, welcome, Ms. Iowa." She was called away to another customer, and Penny stared at her drink. When she looked up she noticed one man, alone, near the drawn vertical blinds of the front window. She hadn't spotted him immediately even though he was the only male in the room, and one of the few nonwhite patrons. His eyes were compelling—though the lighting in the bar made it difficult to identify. Those eyes sent a warm and intrigued greeting to her.

Penny turned away, and found another martini waiting. "From the dude at the window," the bartender said with a wink. Penny realized she was a bit loopy from the drinks, but decided to play the game anyway. What the hell?

Halfway across the room, Penny detoured toward the jukebox as she fished for change and a plan.

"It takes bills too," a silken voice said behind her.

"Thanks," Penny said, and extracted a single. "And thanks for my drink. What do you like? I mean, on the jukebox?" She barely recognized her own voice. Where did that lilt of flirtation come from?

"Why don't I surprise you?" Without delay, he pressed the code into the keypad. "Now it's your turn."

She was momentarily distracted by the warmth in his hazel eyes. "Oh, okay." Penny scanned the playlist and entered the code of a too-familiar tune. Then Hazel Eyes motioned for Penny to follow her.

"So, Spooner probably asked you this, but tell me all about yourself."

"Spooner? Oh, the bartender," Penny said, slowly putting the pieces together.

"She's actually the owner."

"Oh." A faux pas? "Well, I'm new in town. I'm from—"

"Let me guess. Iowa or Missouri or Nebraska. Right?"

"God, you're good. Iowa. How did you know? You're not psychic, are you?"

"No, actually one of my exes was from Iowa."

"One of your exes, eh? And so, do you have a thing for girls from Iowa?"

"I could," Hazel Eyes suggested. "That is, if given the chance." He reached out for Penny's right hand.

As they continued to flirt, Penny's martini sat alone on the counter for about fifteen minutes, which was long enough to annoy Spooner, who took her drink mixing very seriously. She eventually brought the drink over to Penny. Spooner's intrusion broke the spell. "Thanks," Penny said halfheartedly to Spooner, then turned back to Hazel Eyes. She took a sip of the martini and barely noticed how warm it was. "This is probably a mistake. I'd better get going. Thanks again for the drink." She made a halfhearted attempt to look for her cell phone to call for another cab.

"No, wait. We're just getting to know each other. Our songs haven't come on yet," Hazel Eyes pleaded. "Listen, I've got my Jeep outside. I'll drop you off anywhere you want to go."

"Like Canada?"

He smiled.

The next CD flipped onto the jukebox. As soon as the sad Celtic pipes filled the small barroom, Penny realized that she had chosen the extended version. The notes were complicated, discordant at first, but when the violins joined in, they wove together the sounds into a rich harmony. A woman's voice joined with the violins, subtle at first, then clearly articulated into lyrics:

The web of gold encasing my heart is a gilded cage
Tarnished by fear and dusted by pain, but too afraid to escape
Do I dare (do I dare) open the door to you?
(Yes, I see the hope in your eyes.)

Penny rose from the table.

"Wait! We had a deal. Both songs first, right? We have to wait for yours," he said.

What? Penny thought, then smiled self-consciously as the lyrics continued:

Unless I open the door—unless I open my heart
You will never come through.

Hazel Eyes opened his eyes in understanding. They had both chosen the same song. "I get it." He accepted Penny's extended hand and led her toward the minuscule dance floor. "Just one dance." Sighing, she nodded and followed him onto the empty floor. She felt comfortable in his arms and relaxed for the first time.

Near the end of the song they both stopped dancing. Hazel Eyes led her toward the door. This time Penny successfully maneuvered the newspaper obstacles in the doorway, though they did their own twirl when the wind gained entrance from their exit.

* * * * * * * * * * *

Spooner watched them leave as the last words of the verse finished:

But please don't steal, please don't steal
Please, don't
Steal my heart away.

"Uh-huh," Spooner clucked as she was pulled to the end of the bar for a drink order.

Two

Hazel Eyes led Penny to the passenger side of the Jeep, then tilted her head up and bent slightly to kiss her gently on the lips. Penny's return kiss was much more urgent, which changed the intensity of their contact. He quickly recalibrated.

"Wait," Penny said, reluctantly pulling away. "I don't even know your name."

"Marc."

"Nice name," she said breathlessly, and resumed lip-to-lip contact, transgressing with an interplay of tongue.

Marc's apartment was only a few blocks away from the bar. His bedroom faced the same train tracks Penny and the cab driver had followed just an hour—or two?—ago. Marc opened the window; the full light of the moon gilded their bodies with silver. The moonlight was lost in his short, dense hair. Marc undressed Penny, caressing her long, curved body. Penny followed instinctively, unbuttoning Marc's shirt and fumbling the buttons on his Levi's. She marveled in the sheer amazement of her body as she connected with this stranger. Another train passed by, masking the ring of the phone. They never heard either one.

Between kisses Marc asked, "And your name?"

"Penny," she said. Then she sighed.

"I don't like the sound of that," Marc said. "Something bothering you, Penny?"

"I need to come clean," Penny said, conflicted between exploring his body and talking.

"Hey, we're going to play safe," Marc said. "Don't worry, baby."

"No, no, it's not that." Penny sighed again.

"Oh my God," Marc said, and touched her face tenderly. "You know, you are so beautiful when you look sad."

Penny looked at Marc, momentarily stunned, then cleared her thoughts. "I mean, I'm with someone."

Marc stared at her for a moment, maybe ten seconds. "Do you want to be with him?" he asked.

Penny let out another sigh. "I don't think so," she said honestly.

"Do you want to be with me? I mean, right now?" Marc asked.

"Yes. But it's more complicated than that."

"Shhh," he said. "Let's keep this simple. Just this, just us, just now. No other questions." He buried his head in Penny's thick hair.

The doorbell rang just as Penny relaxed into Marc's arms. "Ignore it," Marc whispered between kisses.

It was harder for the both of them to ignore the key in the door.

Three

"Marc!"

"It's Spooner," Marc sighed. "Shhh. I'll deal with this."

With no other explanation, Marc threw on the closest thing he could find, hoping that it and the darkness of the apartment would cover his advanced stage of arousal, and left the room. Penny slid into the bed, as if Spooner had X-ray vision and could see her through the closed door. Even through the door, Penny could hear Spooner as plain as day.

"So, I was talking to some of the girls at the bar," Spooner started, as if it was not odd that she was in Marc's living room in the middle of the night. "They were all quite interested in the hot lady you had just picked up. At first I thought they were being bitchy—that you got to her first. But then they told me a little piece of trivia I thought I'd better share with you."

"Spooner, why are you here? This could have waited until morning. Couldn't you just call me?"

"It is morning. And I knew you wouldn't pick up the phone, especially in the middle of the game. And I figured that it was partially my fault that this happened, seeing that I challenged you to get a home run tonight."

"Spooner, could you be more crass? This isn't the locker room. Stop with the sports lingo, already!" Marc replied, his voice barely audible through the door.

"Oh, sorry, Marc. *Sorry, Ms. Iowa*!" she shouted through the door.

"Ms. Iowa?" Marc asked. Then in a whisper: "Don't tell me I'm trying to bed a beauty queen?" A small smile crept up his lips.

"You are way worse than I thought. No, she's not a beauty queen, so get that Sister Sanguine plot out of your head." Spooner knew she had hit a sensitive point, as only a few souls knew of Marc's addiction to romance novels published by the Sisters Sanguine Press. "This one is better. Way better. But maybe we should have Ms. Iowa tell you that yourself. But I think I'll give you the Cliff's Notes version. *If that's okay with you*," she yelled through the door. She whispered the condensed version; it was over in twenty seconds.

"I know you, Marc," she ended in a quiet voice. "This can't be a good scene. Get her out now, before it goes too far. Listen, I was a jerk tonight. Don't do this because of me."

"Don't worry about me," Marc replied. "I've got it all under control. It's just a spring fling, remember?"

"I bet it is," Spooner muttered as she pulled the door closed behind her.

A few minutes later, Marc walked into the bedroom and turned on a small table lamp. "Well, well. I'm sure you heard that."

"Enough." Penny had at least heard enough to know that there was more than simple friendship between these two. "So you two are—together?" Penny asked.

Marc broke into the loudest, most inelegant laugh jag that Penny had heard in a long time. "Whoa!" he said, nearly hyperventilating. "That would be one for the Springer show!" Settling down, he said, "Sorry—that caught me off guard. I try not to unleash my sexy laugh until after I have gotten to know someone. It's lethal."

Penny laughed too; her laughter was more lyrical. "Spooner is your sister, then, right? Or maybe she's just Spooner to others?"

"No, she's Spooner to everyone, unless you want your ass kicked. She's actually my half sister. Our mother was very, um, prolific with men."

"Is she afraid that the apple doesn't fall too far from the tree?" Penny asked impishly.

Marc winced. "Ouch." He realized that he was probably the polar opposite of his big loving mother, may her soul rest in peace. "Spooner is older than me by one year, a self-appointed guardian angel over me, and gets pissed off when she thinks I am making a fool out of myself." He looked out the dark window. "So the question is this. Am I making a fool of myself?" Marc said this more to himself, then shook his head. "Maybe you'd better tell me who you really are. And I'm sorry I cut you off earlier. It was selfish of me. I wanted to have one perfect night with you before things got complicated."

"And that they are. I'm sorry," Penny said.

"Hey, we all bring in our own complications," Marc added.

"Well," Penny began, "I can't imagine that your life is quite as, uh, conflicted as mine is at the moment."

"What do you mean, Pen?"

In spite of herself, Penny smiled at her new nickname, then sighed. "Well, first of all, I'm not only involved with another man but engaged to him. I also work with him. Actually, we're in a band together."

Marc looked at Penny's now-very-obvious engagement ring. "Spooner said that, among other things. And as for the name of your band, it sounds familiar, but I can't say I recognize it."

Penny bit her tongue. How could she tell Marc that the song they had both selected was the one she and her band, Save the Chukkas, had sent to the top of the pop charts? "Well, basically it's kind of a rock and, uh, has some gospel, uh, undertones." She mumbled through the "gospel" part of the sentence.

"Gospel undertones? You mean, as in Bible and Jerry Falwell kind of stuff?"

She looked at the ceiling. "I'll give you the short version right now, and we'll work our way up to the extended play later. When we started playing music a few years ago, we were classified as an alternative pop band, whatever that means. But when my brother, Benjamin, became our manager, he decided that we'd improve our salability if we stuck to a niche market. As I said, it's a long story. The religious agenda—well, it certainly wasn't my idea or Gary's."

"I assume that Gary is your fiancé?" Marc asked.

"No, actually Lenny is. He's another member of the band. Gary and I are friends. The band, the engagement—it's all a convoluted mess."

Long moments passed. "Marc?" Penny asked, waiting for some reply.

Marc was deep in thought. Finally, he exhaled. "Spooner said that I was sleeping with the enemy. I thought that she meant you were a Republican." He looked at Penny with eyes cleared from the haziness of lust. "Penny—you're name isn't really Penny, is it?"

"My given name is Penelope Lane. My stage name is Margo Steale," she added.

"I see," Marc lied. He didn't understand any of this. All he knew was that the chances of making love to this incredibly beautiful woman had just become statistically negligible. "I guess I deserve this. When I first saw you trip into the bar, I had pegged you for straight and bored with it—which usually spells trouble. Why else would a straight girl go to a dyke bar? And I say that with affection," he added, "since my sister is a hundred percent dyke. After we met, I knew that I was wrong about the experimentation part but still suspected that you could be trouble." Then he stopped with an odd expression on his face.

"Wait. Your name is Penny Lane? Did your parents do that on purpose?"

"My parents have no idea who The Beatles are, so no, they think it's an original." Penny smiled in gratitude for the tension relief but dove back in. "Do you—do you regret tonight?"

"Frankly, I regret we didn't get further," he said, looking down at his lack of erection. "You?"

Penny smiled her answer. "Though it does complicate the hell out of things for me right now."

"Well, I'm glad to hear that," Marc said as he pulled a blanket and pillow from the closet and headed for the couch. "Maybe we can sort it out in the morning. In the meantime, sweet dreams."

Penny watched him leave the room with a surprising amount of regret—regret that they hadn't picked up where they had left off. She wasn't sure if he was taking the couch because of chivalry or lack of interest in her. The honorable thing would have been to leave. But then she remembered the passion she had felt just an hour ago and didn't think she'd been interested in doing the honorable thing just then.

Four

Penny woke up with the all-too-common realization that she couldn't remember where she was. Then, once she did, she had a vague memory of Marc joining her in bed a few hours ago, "I forgot how damn horrible the couch was" his only word of explanation before he fell sound asleep. The telltale signs of his presence included the rumpling of the sheets on the left side of the bed. She heard the dampened sounds of cabinets and china; she assumed Marc was making coffee or breakfast. She chose to stay in bed. After looking at the books on Marc's bedside table (aha, here was the answer to Spooner's "Sisters Sanguine" reference last night), she reached for the phone to retrieve her voice mail messages from her downtown condo.

The first message was from Gary the night before: "I'm coming over after Jaime and Gus start loading the bus. Should be there about midnight. See ya then. By the way, good job in pissing Benji off. Because you weren't there to cover his fat ass, he didn't have time to prepare his words for the altar call. He only netted four souls for the kingdom." Then a second call from Gary: "Penny, I just tried your place, but you weren't there. Maybe we got our wires crossed. I thought I was going to come over and talk about this engagement thing. Really, Penny, we need to talk. Lenny is not the one for you. I'll call you tomorrow—well, I guess it is tomorrow already. Shit. Never mind."

Then Lenny: "Where are you, baby? We were supposed to register at Macy's this morning. Call me. I'm worried about you, especially after last night."

If he only knew the half of it, Penny mused.

Last, her brother, Benjamin: "I am very disappointed in your behavior last night, sis. I mean, really, what were you thinking about?" For a moment Penny thought that he was referring to her failed one-nighter with Marc, and wondered how the hell he knew. Then he droned on: "No one was the wiser that you had left the concert in a foulmouthed huff. And, praise Jesus, no reporters were around to hear you. That would have been a publicity disaster. The *Sun Times* even has a nice write-up about us. That wouldn't have happened if they had heard you last night. You've got to think, girl—"

"What an asshole," Penny muttered as she hung up on Benjamin's message.

"Good morning, Ms. Steale." Marc walked in wearing a pair of silk pajama bottoms; his chest showed recent evidence of precipitation: either a walk in a rainstorm or a shower. "These are yours, I presume?" He handed Penny her clothes, warm from the dryer.

"Thanks," Penny said, not moving. "Marc, I'm sorry about last night. Maybe this all was a mistake. I really didn't mean to create a fuss with your friends and all."

Marc sat at the end of the bed. "Is this the kiss-off speech?"

"What? No, no," Penny replied. She decided her hesitation to dress in front of him was bordering on pathology and peeled the bedding from her body. "I just assumed that you wouldn't want anything to do with me after you knew about the band. I mean, I'm not sure if we can be, well, you know—"

"Fuck buddies?" Marc's response even surprised himself. "Gee, I should probably not hang out with lesbians so much—I start talking like them."

Penny hesitated as she hooked her bra. "That's not quite what I was going to say, but in a crude way, I guess it's what I meant. Actually, I'm not really sure what I mean. In the meantime, can we be friends?"

He rolled his eyes. "Sure, whatever." He watched Penny slide into her tight jeans. "But I can't promise that we won't move on to other things. I felt some heat last night, and unless I am completely mistaken, it wasn't all from me. You fascinate me, Ms. Steale, a.k.a. Penny Lane. By the way, do you know that you're in the paper?"

Penny didn't really hear his comment at first, as she was too busy watching Marc watch her. She barely noticed that she was working her jeans back off, and that he was helping her. Unfortunately, the doorbell rang, and they both sighed in futility as Penny pulled her jeans on.

Five

At the door was a neighbor's son who wanted to sell chocolates for his middle school band fund-raising. Rotten luck, Marc thought as he forked over ten dollars for the candy.

Over coffee he showed her the *Sun Times* article he printed off their Web site:

Bluer Skies Ahead?

Fans of Save the Chukkas gave them a welcome that they themselves were not quite prepared for. Admittedly, the band performed better during their opening concert here four months ago, but they did conjure up the frenzied atmosphere that set the Family First Church rocking during their three-hour concert as they finished their multimillion-dollar "Steale Away"concert tour.

The surprise star of the show—and of the tour itself—was Lenny Blue, who, even at the end of the tour, was as vibrant and fresh as during his rousing debut at this year's Grammy Awards. Even lead singer Margo Steale could not outlast the exuberance of the Blue Man; the band, sans Steale, took four encores. Gary

Davis, lead guitarist, left the audiences wild with his artistic rhythms and dance. But even so, he lagged at the end, outshined by Blue.

Even with their fatigued performance, Save the Chukkas, with the gritty and compelling voice of Steale, the musicianship and charisma of Blue and the wild-child passion of Davis, are a formidable band as the sky is their limit. Perhaps their manager, Benjamin Lane, should take a lesson from this and let the band play inside a little less and play outside a little more. The message here, Lane? Let them rest on their laurels.

Marc stared at her. "I feel pretty stupid that I didn't know who you were," he admitted. "But maybe I know your music." He looked wide-eyed at her, nodding at her in encouragement. "Sing something."

Penny knew she should fess up about the song but couldn't bring herself to do it. "This isn't *American Idol.* I can't sing this early in the morning, Marc. God, I rarely am up this early. Really," she replied to Marc's embarrassment, "it's not a big deal."

"A Grammy is not a big deal?"

"Well, sure it is. But I have a theory about this."

Marc smiled. He recognized a rationalization when he saw one. "From the looks of this," he said, referring to the review, "you greatly underestimate your band's talent."

Penny blushed. "I think we're good. But under normal circumstances I doubt we could compete with the political clout of the Nashville religious royalty. I think Benjamin somehow rigged the votes by calling in favors. Anyway, I see you were busy surfing the Net," she said as she noticed other articles on the kitchen table.

"Oh yeah. I've found out a bit about you. You'll be happy to know that your story checks out. So far." Marc sipped his coffee. "You know, this is the first time I ever had to check out a potential date via the Internet. Ms. Steale, you have been truly an educational experience."

To her credit, Penny took Marc's comments with humor. "My pleasure, Mr.—"

"Hawthorne," Marc said. "I see we haven't been properly introduced. Marc Hawthorne," he said, shaking Penny's hand. "And you are the infamous lead Chukka, who hails from the fair but uneventful state of Iowa."

"Charmed, I'm sure. But please call me Penny. Anything else you wanna know before Spooner beats me to it?"

"Hmmm." Marc tapped a finger to his lips. "I think I know something about you that you don't know."

"Really?"

"Apparently last night wasn't the first time you went AWOL from your band, that you usually let the guys finish the encores for you. The press has speculated about that."

"And the surprise here? I'm sick of Benny's altar calls. I told him that if he stops, I will stop leaving before the encores."

"Well, the press doesn't know that. And when they don't understand, they fabricate. I'm sure you've heard some of the theories—that you have a hidden illness or that you are giving the stage to your fiancé so that he can have his time in the spotlight."

"Or that I'm a closet drug user and use the time to score some coke from the dealers in the audience," Penny added. "One of my personal favorites."

"I missed that one. Anyway, another theory has emerged, this time from *Chicago Lives*, one of the finest examples of journalistic garbage to come to our fair city in years." Marc could barely contain his contempt for the publication.

"Can't wait." Penny lifted orange juice to her lips.

"Apparently, they have tracked this unusual behavior of yours for a while now. They calculate that you are now about four weeks pregnant, and are suffering from 'evening sickness,' which their 'medical expert' sites as a phenomenon for those who have atypical work and sleep schedules."

Marc could not go on, as a fine spray of OJ hit him in the face.

Penny apologized and ran for the paper towels. "God, I'm sorry. I haven't done that since lunchroom days."

"No, thank *you*," Marc said. "Good thing I blinked."

They made plans for later that evening. "Are you sure you want to try this?" Marc referred to their ambiguous relationship.

"Hmmm," Penny replied, "I think we may have to work up to the 'fuck buddy' stage, but for now"—she pulled Marc in for a long kiss—"yeah, I'm sure." She walked out the door, then turned back around. "What about you, Marc? What would I find if I looked for you on the web?"

Marc smiled enigmatically. "Go do your homework. Maybe you'll find out you're sleeping with the enemy too."

* * * * * * * * * * *

The sky over Lake Michigan was perfect, cloudless. Penny barely noticed as the cab sped south along Lake Shore Drive. The reality of the previous evening—and of her new infatuation—was beginning to sink in.

The cab turned down Michigan Avenue and eventually dropped Penny on Pearson Street across from Loyola's law school. Students were rushing to and from the school's library. Penny watched a woman in a white pickup truck drive away, rainbow sticker adorning the bumper. She thought of her accidental foray into a lesbian bar the previous night, and the impossible connection with a fascinating man. *God, what am I in for?* she mused.

The phone was ringing when Penny walked into her condo. Without thinking she picked it up. "Hello?"

"Penny, what the hell is going on?"

"What?" Penny replied. Who was calling her, Gary or Lenny? Sometimes they sounded the same on the phone. "Uh, Gary?" She hoped.

"I would think you would recognize your fiancé's voice by now."

Shit. "Oh, hi, Lenny. I'm sorry. I got delayed."

"Well, hurry up. We've got to do this today. People are starting to complain they don't know what to buy us."

"Listen, Lenny, something's come up and I'll need to cancel." Penny dropped her purse and jacket on her white canvas couch. God, she hated that couch.

"You mean reschedule our appointment?" Lenny asked. "God, sweetie, do you not listen? We can't put this stuff off much longer, or there won't be a wedding."

"Well, we'll just have to talk about that, won't we?" Penny said, and hung up. The phone rang again; she didn't bother answering it but instead shed her clothes in the white living room on the way to the white bathroom. She adjusted the water temperature, then sent it streaming from the tub faucet to the showerhead and slowly entered the spray.

What would have happened had she just come back to the apartment last night? Penny wondered as she rinsed the shampoo out of her hair and reached for the conditioner. She would no doubt have argued with Gary about her future with Lenny. And she would never have met Marc, whose mere existence provided Penny with a complicated but delicious distraction.

Penny reached for the razor and took great care to trace the gentle curves of her ankles, her knees, and all the way up her thighs, remembering how Marc had touched these very places the evening before. It was too bad Spooner and then the band kid interrupted them, Penny mused as she finished rinsing the shaving cream off her legs and opened the glass doors.

Lenny Blue sat on the edge of the sink, watching. "Hello, baby," he said without blinking.

"Why are you in here? Do you have any sense of decency?" Penny knew she sounded like her mother.

"Oh, come on, Prissy Penelope, we're going to be married in a month. It's not like we haven't 'done it.'" Lenny emphasized the "done it" with finger quotations.

She grabbed a towel and wondered when the hell he had picked up that annoying habit. "Get out."

Lenny smirked, then closed the door behind him. He yelled through the bathroom door: "Okay, if you want to play games. I'll be downstairs in the restaurant. We'll talk there." Ten seconds later he slammed the front door.

Penny left the bathroom and walked to her bedroom, keeping the towel wrapped around her just in case he hadn't really left. "Damn it!" she whispered. She had been fighting the reality of it for months, but the events of the last day provided instant clarity. As she lay on the bed, Penny realized exactly what she needed to do.

Six

Benjamin was waiting with Lenny at the restaurant. This was not a big surprise to Penny. Benjamin and Lenny had tended to shadow each other the last few months. Lenny had the same damn smirk on his face when she reached their table. Upstairs, Penny had thought that it represented lust; here, she read it as a form of sadism.

"Sis," Benjamin said as she sat down, "we've ordered already, but the waiter will be coming back if you 'want' something." He drew quotations around the word "want" with his fingers.

Penny wondered again for the thousandth time if slamming his fingers in a car door would fix that proclivity; now he had Lenny doing the same thing. "I'm fine. Just tell me what's going on." She was starving, but there was no way she would encourage extended time with these guys. She just needed to say what she had to say and get the hell out of there.

"I'm a little 'concerned,' honey," Benjamin said, grabbing some bread from the basket with meaty fingers. Benjamin's voice, normally loud, took on a false singsong nature. Penny knew he had chosen his "pastoral" approach. He never ceased to remind her that though he was the band's manager, he was first and foremost an ordained minister. "Now," he continued, "I know that you have a foul mouth at times—I blame Gary's influence for that—but you were way out of line last night. If I didn't think something deeper was going on, I would expect an apology."

Lenny's smirk had been replaced by a look of concern. "Benjamin, don't be too hard on her. I mean, the stress of a wedding can really be tough on—"

"The little filly," Penny said, completing his thought.

"Penny, that's not where I was going. I'm not sexist." Lenny had the forethought to look wounded.

Penny avoided looking at both of them. "Guys, I'm sorry, but I can't get into this particular issue with you now. I was up late last night—"

"Yeah, where were you?" Benjamin asked. Then, in a whisper, "Are you using drugs'?"

"God, Benji." she said, refusing even to acknowledge the question with an answer. Though she did hit the bull's-eye, calling him his childhood name and taking the Lord's name in vain in one fell swoop.

The waiter brought their food. Penny noticed Benjamin's attention lingering on the waiter as he walked away.

"Unrepentant homosexuals," Benjamin said as he bit into his sandwich. "Can't they go somewhere else to work?"

Penny felt her face was on fire. "Benjamin, will you keep your closed-minded, archaic notions to yourself?"

"A few came up last night," added Lenny.

"What!" Penny shouted, then adjusted her voice. "You didn't give an altar call for gays to get healed, did you?"

"What could I do? The Lord just 'put' it on my heart, and I had to say it. I didn't want to 'quench' the Spirit," Benjamin replied.

"Come on, Penny, why have you resisted this?" Lenny added. "Of course God can heal gays. He can heal alcoholics and drug abusers, why not sexual deviants?"

"Go ahead, become the next Jimmy Swaggart," she said as she pushed away from the table. "I don't care. But I have been clear all along I don't buy all that mumbo-jumbo born-again crap. Maybe the two of you do. Great. Maybe you should get married. Oh yeah, you can't, can you? That would be a damnable sin."

Lenny looked at Benjamin. Benjamin said in a stage whisper, "Maybe a demon is 'contending' for her soul."

"Benjamin, you don't even talk like you belong in this fucking century." Penny got up. "I've said too much, and unfortunately it's all true. But just in case it isn't clear, Lenny, the wedding's off. Benjamin, I want out of my contract. Pronto."

As Penny walked away she heard Benjamin say, "This is Gary's fault. He's done corrupted her."

Seven

And then Penny woke up from her nap. "Shit," she said, after she realized her conversation with Lenny and Ben was only woven in her dreams. "Well, there's nothing better than a dress rehearsal," she said to her empty bed.

Trying to fight the déjà vu, she entered the restaurant downstairs. No Benjamin; only Lenny waited for her. That blew the reenactment. Oh well, it was probably better this way, she told herself. She wasn't convinced.

"Sweetie," Lenny said, rising from his seat. Unlike the dream, and his momentary lapse upstairs in her bathroom, deep down Lenny was a gentleman, even when she kept him waiting. As she walked over to his table, Penny's eyes traced his familiar face as if touching a worry stone. Short straw-colored hair, a straight nose, a mustache and goatee framing a generous mouth not prone to laughter. Lenny's hazel eyes were circled by small gold wire glasses, and he looked thinner than usual under his brown turtleneck sweater and black jeans. He had been a comforting presence in her life, up to the engagement. Since then, that comfort had metamorphosed into something Penny only now recognized as need.

Penny realized that it was the hazel eyes that did her in. They were a similar shade to Marc's. She hoped that was where the similarities ended.

Lenny began speaking. "Hey, I'm sorry about upstairs. I'm not sure why I did that." He blushed slightly as he held out her chair. "You are very beautiful. I keep seeing you, uh, well, and it's hard to erase—" In his own screwed-up way, he was sincere.

Penny let him take his seat before she blurted out her confession. "Len, you know I have treasured these last two years and have loved you for the dear friend you are, but I—I don't love you the way a wife should love a husband."

Lenny looked at her blankly. "Penny, don't you know that I understand that?"

"What?" Penny was confused. She took a sip of water with trembling hands. "You knew that I wasn't in love with you? Then why did you go along with this?"

Lenny looked at her desperately. "Because. Because we had to. Because it's God's will."

This was certainly not turning out like the dream. Nor was any of it making sense. Penny attempted to add a little levity to the bizarre turn of events. "Did God tell you something that He didn't tell me?"

"Never mind," he said, apparently not in the mood for humor.

"Lenny, this is serious. We were scheduled to get married next month. Why would you allow this to go on if you knew I didn't love you that way?"

Lenny was good about turning the question around. "Why did you? You're an adult. You can take responsibility for at least half of this."

At least half? thought Penny. Who proposed to whom? "Lenny, I just figured this out, I mean, about marrying you. It happened so quickly, with the Grammy and everything. And then I guess that I was so tired from the concerts that I didn't have a chance to think about what this meant." She took his hand. "Len, can I ask you this? Did you love me? Like a lover? Or like a friend?"

He shrugged. "Who can know that? And anyway, I figured if nothing else we'd grow to love each other. Romance is a relatively recent luxury, you know."

With that statement, Penny knew that she was doing the right thing. "Listen, we're both tired." At least she knew she was. "Maybe we should talk more later. But I do know I cannot marry you. It wouldn't be fair to either one of us."

She expected a fight, or something, but Lenny was silent. Finally, exhaling loudly, Lenny nodded sadly. "Okay. You win." More silence. Then: "Can we wait to announce this? I would—I would like to tell my folks first before …" He stared at his lap for a long time.

Penny could tell he struggled with an inner dialogue she was not privy to. "Lenny, this is not about you. I love you. But not enough. I think you deserve someone who loves you in a way that I can't." Did that ever sound cliché?

"I have no investment in how this looks," she continued, not sure what particular pain was troubling him most: the loss of love or of ego. "If you want to tell people that I broke this off, fine. Whatever you need to say, do it."

Lenny looked at her with troubled eyes. His expression broke her heart. "Sweetie," Penny said, "you know I'm right. We can't go through with the marriage. If you've ever loved deeply before—and I would guess you have, because I know you and your poet's soul—you know I'm right." She knew that this conversation could go on all day and still go no further. Ending it now was the humane thing to do.

Lenny's eyes stayed in his lap. No words would comfort him now. She knew he needed to be the last one to leave. Penny held him from behind for a minute, then left. She wondered how long he would sit there.

Penny rode the elevator upstairs alone. Even with a heavy heart, she couldn't help comparing Lenny's body with Marc's.

Lenny and she were almost the same size. On the occasions when they engaged in affection for each other (they had been, after all, engaged), they were clumsy; his body parts would collide with her coinciding parts. In contrast, Marc's touch energized her like no other man's before.

* * * * * * * * * *

Lenny watched Penny walk out of the restaurant. He had hoped this day would never come. In one way, it was inevitable. It was both and neither of their faults. They had both known.

Lenny signaled for the check and pulled out his wallet. As he fumbled for a credit card, he accidentally drew out a condom. He and Penny had almost used that condom the previous weekend in Wisconsin. He pushed the package back out of sight.

It had been one of those rare free days when Benjamin had allowed them a day off. They had played in a large stadium in Madison and they stayed in the guest rooms at the student union of the University of Wisconsin's main campus. Benjamin and Gary had both discovered and pursued their own agendas: Benjamin visited a pastor friend he had gone to college with; Gary was on the lookout for some local brews and a little action. Amazingly, Lenny and Penny were left alone. After eating at one of the Middle Eastern restaurants on State Street where they had both had a little too much to drink, they walked back to the Student Union's terrace, lightly holding hands.

They were not the only ones who appreciated the warmth of the remarkable March evening. A few dozen people sat at the small metal tables. A sunset set off the evening, the fiery ball briefly reflected in Lake Mendota, then extinguished by the green hills around them. They relaxed in the tranquil notes of the live music, a local band that had a pretty big draw.

Later, she invited him into her room. He hesitated, then walked over the threshold and shut the door behind him.

"Penny?" In his voice was a question, a need. Perhaps he wanted her to say no. Instead she pulled him to her, where they shared kisses, caresses. They moved from the doorway to her bed, where they lay down and touched. Lenny was suddenly aware of a passion that he had never known with a woman before. Impatiently, he didn't bother with a condom and entered her quickly. Yet, after his urgency passed, he looked at Penny's face and did not see the desire. She was going through the motions. They eventually stopped like a car out of gas, bodies disengaging. "Penny?" he asked again.

She looked at him earnestly, then began to dress. Long moments passed. "I wanted this too. But I couldn't be there with you," she said. "I don't know why the hell not, but I couldn't." Penny then stared out the window, unwilling or unable to articulate her thoughts any further. Eventually Lenny left, returning to an empty room with confused thoughts that did not diminish.

Lenny shook the previous week's memory from his mind as a waiter returned to his table. He signed the credit card receipt. He tucked his copy away in his billfold and sat for a moment longer. Three thoughts bombarded him in quick succession.

First, Lenny realized that Penny's words in the hotel room had nothing at all to do with propriety and everything to do with honesty.

Second, he knew Penny was right: he had loved her more as a friend than he could ever as a husband.

And third, Lenny knew an attractive Latino man seated across the dining room was calling him over to his table with dark brown eyes, and now nothing held him back.

Eight

Spooner woke in a foul mood. After reviewing the unpleasant little episode last night at Marc's—when she found out that Marc was harboring that wannabe dyke—Spooner was in the mood for some pain and headed off to the gym. Marc had really pissed her off this time, and she needed to get it out of her system before she started work and took it out on her customers. Not good for business.

Not that the bar didn't give Spooner a workout. Yet when the extent of her movement entailed lifting liquor bottles, shaking drinks, pulling the tab … this in no way rivaled a Nautilus machine. At least this was what Spooner's friend Jordan said. Jordan owned the gym. After months of arm twisting, Jordan had persuaded Spooner to join. And since it was just two blocks away from Spooner's place, she had little excuse not to go.

Besides, there were quite a few lookers at the gym.

Since then, Spooner had consistently gone four days a week, more if she had opportunity or in this case, need. Spooner knew it made quite a difference in her game. Sex had never been better.

Spooner thought she knew why Jordan was so insistent. Jordan was afraid Spooner had forgotten all about being a sister. She was afraid that Spooner was hanging around the white girls too much. It was a battle they'd fought since the beginning of their friendship in grammar school.

In Spooner's eyes, Jordan was always a bit of a crusader. The gym was one of her most recent crusades. It provided an oasis of color in the midst of Chicago's North Side Andersonville neighborhood, where ethnicity included anything Scandinavian such as lutefisk and a blond white girl dressed as St. Lucia parading down Clark Street with a goose and a head full of candles during high Christmas shopping season. Jordan once commented: "White folks' traditions can be pretty ridiculous, if you ask me. You don't see any of us black folk walking around with Kwanzaa candles sticking out of our heads. What's the point?"

Jordan. Always the practical one.

As much as she gave Jordan a hard time about her participation at the gym, Spooner secretly enjoyed working out. The gym was filled with some of the typical exercise machines—rowing, stair climbers, treadmills—but it was a place to build muscle. Weight machines for upper and lower body, torso sculpting, bodybuilding. Classes for self-defense and boxing rounded out the offerings. It was a serious, no-bullshit place. No leotards or thongs. Nothing pastel survived long in Jordan's gym.

When Spooner arrived at the gym that morning, she avoided Jordan and all three of the other members present. Choosing the higher end of the weight spectrum, she straddled a machine and started to lift.

"Girl, you better warm up first." Jordan approached her friend. "What's wrong with you?"

"Get off me!" Spooner already felt the strain in her back.

Jordan recoiled, put her hands out. "Backing off!" she replied, and walked away. She knew when Spooner was in a mood. Any reprimands would go in one ear and out the other.

With the pain growing, Spooner thought more about the scene at Marc's. "What an ass!" she hissed, exhaling. She wasn't sure if she was referring to Marc or herself. Spooner hated pitching fits. "What a fucking soap opera," she added, exhaling again as she released the weight, then inhaling as she pulled. She could still see Marc, trying to wipe that goofy look of infatuation off his face. Like a kid that just got caught doing something stupid. Spooner knew right then it was too late to warn him. He'd already stuck his finger in the honey pot, figuratively if not literally.

"Hey!" Jordan reappeared at Spooner's side. "Are you even counting your reps?"

"Yeah," she lied.

"The hell you are. You're doing too much, too fast, and without warming up. If you're mad, go punch the bag. Don't take it out by slamming my weights." She rubbed Spooner's back. "You're a rock. You're gonna tear everything out back there."

Spooner changed the subject. "Where's everyone?"

"Saturday. It's always dead in here. Everyone's at brunch eating fucking frittata or something. You're never in to notice."

Spooner knew this was a little jab at the frequency of her sexual conquests. She realized that Jordan and Marc were not unalike in some ways.

"Spoon, what's up? It's Marc again, isn't it? No one else seems to get you quite as riled up."

She'll get it out of me anyway, Spooner thought. *Might as well spill it*. "You heard of Margo Steale?" She let go of the weights.

Jordan scratched her bald head. "Pop star? Gospel singer?"

"All of the above. She came into the bar last night. Marc picked her up."

Jordan laughed. "He's got his hands full with that one."

"The little shit. He's in love with a white, fundamentalist pop star! I tried talking with him, but he's too far gone already. The worst is, he doesn't know he is."

"Why do you care so much?" Jordan asked. "He's an adult. What's riding you? That she's white and beautiful or that she sings about Jesus?"

"Are you nuts? My little brother dating someone like her? How can he reconcile the politics of it all?"

"Well, that's interesting," Jordan said, trailing the thought across the room. She didn't have to finish it. Spooner knew what Jordan thought. They had had this kind of conversation only a million times already. Usually Spooner's response was more establishment than Jordan's; now the tables had turned.

"Why don't you hit the sauna?" Jordan yelled. "That'll help you more than busting up my weights."

Again, always the practical one, Spooner mused as she wiped down her machine and headed for the locker room.

Nine

Marc had never seen Spooner quite as upset with him. It wasn't as if they didn't have plenty of things to fight about. Being siblings created its own life complications. Choosing to enter a business relationship created a new level of tension.

Marc knew he couldn't blame Spooner; he knew she could be particularly stubborn and opinionated if she wanted to; they both shared that genetic trait from their mother. Guzzling lukewarm coffee left over from Penny's abandoned mug, Marc couldn't help wondering if the stars had gotten him in trouble last night

He had been in a particularly reckless mood, something a former lover, Dale Sentry, would have called "full moon frenzy." It was a particularly clear night, even with the wind blowing as it was, and Marc could have pointed out a few of the constellations he had been teaching his students about in class just that week. Pretty remarkable for a Chicago night.

On top of it all, it was not just any Friday night, but the beginning of spring break. On a normal Friday night, Marc would have worked on lesson plans, or finished some tasks around the home. But for some reason he was feeling a bit reckless, more like a student than a teacher, and let it all slide and went to Spooner's.

If he'd been trying to get lucky, going to Spooner's bar was Marc's biggest tactical error. Even though it was his favorite bar (an admitted bias since he had a vested financial interest in the place), he had never connected with women there. Not surpising, since it was a lesbian bar. He was often the token (in gender and ethnically), except for the occasional neophyte gay man who would wander in thinking that it was a mixed bar. It wasn't. This had much to do with Spooner, and her appeal in the rainbow-loving world of the feminine gender.

Spooner was a celebrity, at least in the women-loving-women set on the North Side. Though relatively low-key in comparison with her friend Jordan, Spooner was still an active and visible force in the local lesbian scene. She was also a brilliant artist. Her subjects were nudes of the female variety. Most of Spooner's lovers became subjects, or vice versa.

However, with ever masochistic hope for a Grace to accompany a Will, Marc had driven the few blocks to the bar.

Spooner was at the counter, looking over her realm as if she were a proud drag king, her white sleeveless T-shirt highlighting arms revealing promise of more curve and muscle underneath the shirt. Her pale blue jeans were tight and worn low on her hips. Though Marc couldn't see them from here, she assumed Spooner was wearing her burgundy penny loafers. Instead of pennies, she had widened the slits to accommodate a Sacagawea coin for each shoe.

Marc sidled up to the bar. "Coke, straight up," he said. He was not much of a drinker.

"Lightweight," she responded. Neither of them drank much; Marc because he liked his inhibitions too much to lose them, and Spooner because drinking cut into her profits. Spooner squirted out the drink into a highball glass to give the drink an appearance of iniquity. "How's laundry?"

Marc wasn't sure if the fresh scent of Downy gave him away, or the knowledge gleaned from years of predictability. Friday was laundry night. "I've washed my sheets, just in case—"

Spooner rolled her eyes. "Here's what I don't get about you. You act as if you really want to meet someone, but then you doom yourself by hanging out at a queer bar."

"But I like it here." He shrugged. "And you know my theory. If it's the right girl, she can just as easily walk right through that door—"

"And run right out screaming," Spooner said. "Besides, I should leave you alone. You're good to have around. Kind of like the bar pet. Like a cute, cuddly little puppy or kitty cat."

He frowned. "That's great to know. I'm glad that my reputation as a stud muffin is so well defended here. Where is everyone tonight?"

"At the benefit. That's where the action is."

"Well, I guess you'll be scraping tonight too." Marc knew Spooner's dance card wasn't always full, but he liked to ride Spooner about it as much as she framed Marc's life in monkish predictability.

"You could always go downtown," Spooner said, referring to the Blue Vista Ball at the Old Starlight Hotel. "I doubt the party's over." She started her bartender impression and wiped a ring of Coke off the counter left from Marc's drink. She was very neat in her kingdom. Her apartment was another matter altogether. "I'm sure that there are some token straights there. You may run into Dale, talk about old times."

"No, thanks." Marc rolled his eyes. Black-tie events made him feel itchy. "Don't look at me like that. I support Blue Vista." Marc bought two of the two-hundred-dollar tickets and promptly gave them to his friend D2. D2 was working on his taxes. He would never take money outright, since he asserted that he was already making a tidy sum with his practice, and since he was not a CPA but a lawyer.

"Okay, truce," she said, shaking Marc's hand, giving in a bit too prematurely.

One of the clientele asked Spooner to change a twenty for her. Spooner did just that, but whispered something into her ear as she pulled another buck from the cash register. The customer smiled and took the bill from Spooner. Immediately Marc knew what was coming.

The money was fed into the jukebox. The woman punched her selections, and she clomped back to her seat. Within fifteen seconds, Marc's worst nightmare was realized.

Patsy Cline was singing "Walking After Midnight." A few chuckles; one or two fingers pointed at Marc.

Spooner set the song up practically every time Marc came into the bar. It was Spooner's commentary on her brother's fantasy of finding a straight girl at a dyke bar. It was harmless ribbing and usually Marc let it slide. But because he had been hoping for some magic before entering the bar, he took up the gauntlet. Not only was he going to take someone home tonight, but he was going to do it right in front of Spooner so there would be no doubt. Squinting his eyes in determination, Marc rose from the bar with a freshened Coke and waited at a table for his prey.

Of course, no one entered the bar for a long time after that. Even so, it was a ridiculous challenge on his part. Marc was getting ready to give up after his seventh Coke and third trip to the bathroom when a woman walked in. And not just any woman.

Penny.

Penny was an Amazon; maybe five feet nine—only a few inches short than him. Dark blond hair. Lots of it. Tan skin, even so early in the season. Warm brown eyes sweeping over a strong, straight nose and high cheekbones. A confident, hip-accentuating stride.

But it was when Penny stumbled into the bar, tripping over the newspapers, that Marc was smitten. He had a soft spot in his heart for klutzes.

Of course he hadn't known Penny was Penny then. What Marc did know was at that precise moment this woman stopped being a potential fling, his way to get back at Spooner, his attempt to win a bet.

Sipping what was moving from tepid to iced coffee, Marc fast-forwarded to the scenes in his apartment early that morning. Marc had barely heard Penny's confessions when Spooner forced herself into his living room. That was the first time. The second time was just moments after Penny had left.

Spooner had had the courtesy to knock the second time around, though Marc regretted opening the door the moment Spooner opened her mouth. "White girls are hard enough," Spooner had said as she stood in the doorway. "Fundies are far worse. First they convert you, and then they break your heart." Spooner was never one who took her time speaking her mind.

"You don't know Penny. She's not a fundy. Besides, I am not in love with her. God, we just met. You are being silly."

"We'll see who's being silly," Spooner said, and after several more sample expletives and predictions of doom, shut the door firmly behind her.

After finishing his coffee, Marc had changed the sheets. Maybe Spooner was right, he mused as he pulled the fitted sheet off the mattress. Though Marc always thought he calculated his risks when it came to love, he was often shown to be the fool. This time he knew he was being less than rational, very unscientific in his approach. Foolishly, he found comfort in this. In a strange way, it was refreshing to find out the dirt at the beginning of an affair instead of at the end. What else could happen to make it worse? Marc didn't want to worry about that right now. He realized that he was clutching the sheets and flung them in the hamper.

Marc found Penny's phone number during his computer search. Impulsively, he dialed the number and left a message, which he instantly regretted. Really, how far could one go with a woman who sang about God?

Spooner was probably right.

Ten

Marc was momentarily stunned by Penny's beauty. All he could do was stare when Penny opened the door. Unlike the night before, she wore a breezy cotton dress that clung and flowed in all the right places. She still wore her red boots.

"You wanna come in, or just stand there all night?"

Marc walked in and pushed the door shut behind her. "I'm trying to remember if I'm just a friend or a lover. If I'm a friend, I can give you a hug, but not a wet kiss on the lips."

"Let's just see what happens," Penny said as she kissed him and swept him through the door. She gave him a quick tour of the condo. "This is actually the band's condo, but I get to live here." She didn't sound overjoyed by the honor. "Benjamin decided we needed a clean, professional look—it's all about business," she commented on the contemporary but bland canvas furniture. Marc knew it cost a lot more than it looked.

"You do have a remarkable view," Marc added, looking out her kitchen window over a slice of the Loop. The Chicago River snaked between formidable buildings and under countless bridges showcasing different architectural styles and eras. "I might be tempted to cook more if I had a view like this."

Penny encircled him from behind with strong, tan arms; his arms held hers; he liked the way her bronze and his brown arms looked together. He realized he was in deeper than he thought.

"The problem with windows is that not only can we look out, but people can look in." Penny withdrew her arms. "Hey, I'm starving," she said, and pulled Marc away from the kitchen.

Penny had made reservations at her building's penthouse restaurant. "Not the one downstairs," she added as they walked out the door, which made no sense to Marc. It did shortly. After they were seated at their table, Penny told Marc about her talk with Lenny at the downstairs restaurant.

"You did what?" Marc said, almost choking on a bread stick the diameter of a half centimeter.

"I broke off the engagement." As if to prove it, she showed Marc her ringless finger, complete with tan line.

Marc wasn't sure whether to do cartwheels or panic, and he silently recited a mantra that Spooner was convinced lowered blood pressure. "Uh, wow. Is this because of last night? I mean, I didn't mean for you to rush anything."

"But Marc, it was clear. I didn't love him. I mean, not like that. I think I knew that before, but it took something like last night to hit me over the head."

Dummy, Marc said to himself, *she's not asking you to marry her. Just go with it.* Out loud and in a calm voice he asked, "And how do you feel about this?" using words he recognized as Dale's, his ex-girlfriend, the therapist.

"Great! I mean, I feel bad for Lenny, and so I feel a bit guilty that I feel so relieved about it. But it's the best thing for both of us." She took a bite of salad. "You know, it's strange, but I think that he was more excited about the idea of being married than he was getting married to me. Isn't that weird?"

"Well—"

Penny cut Marc off. "I mean, it was like he needed to be married. When I pressed him on that, he wouldn't talk. Weird." She shook her head, then continued on her salad.

Marc noticed a change in her. Penny's face was relaxed, radiant, the nervous tension melting with the setting sun. It reminded him of the innocence he had encountered outside the Jeep and in bed.

Penny caught Marc off guard. "What were you just thinking about?"

Marc felt himself blush. "Oh, about last night. About how, well, how lovely you were in the moonlight. Sorry." He wondered if Penny thought the declaration was as corny as he found it.

"Not at all." Penny smiled. "But I had just asked you a question and I knew that you weren't even paying attention."

"Pen," Marc started, "what are you going to do now that you've broken the engagement? Won't it be awkward to work in the band together?"

She lowered the fork from her mouth. "I haven't thought too much about that. I hope that we can be adults about it all. If not, then, I guess time will tell."

"Do you have a videotape, you know, of the Grammys? When you won?"

"No. Okay, yes. I'm so bad at lying. It's just, well, that's where Lenny proposed. I don't care to see that for a good long time, if ever again."

"He proposed to you on TV? In front of millions of people?" Marc stared in amazement. "No wonder why you accepted. What else could you have done?"

"It was a bit coercive, wasn't it?" she mused. "Never mind that. Can I see your classroom sometime? I hear it's incredible."

Marc laughed. Penny must have been surfing the Net. "So you have been doing your homework. Sure. But first, I would like to see something else."

"Don't say my Grammy tape!"

Marc didn't say a word. Penny got the message. "Waiter, check please," they both said at the same time. Just like in the movies.

Eleven

Marc had heard accounts of people making love in an elevator before, and dismissed those stories as silly and unrealistic. Suddenly he understood all too well. They barely made it to the elevator before they began reaching for each other. Halfway down, Marc finally articulated his question: "Does this mean we've moved on from friends to lovers?"

Penny hesitated, then smiled. "Naw. From friends to fuck buddies. What did you think?" she asked, kissing Marc deeply.

Marc freed his mouth and whispered in her ear, "Just wanted to ask. To make sure I was catching the subtle hints."

They reached Penny's floor; the elevator door opened in a tumble of arms and kisses. Penny fumbled for her key; Marc's nibbles hampered her speed. Penny found the key and they slid in, quickly closing the door. They didn't bother with the light; the lights from the neighboring buildings lit up the room. Their movements were fluid, undulating. Just as Marc reached to unbutton Penny's shirt, he felt a chill. Penny froze.

"Well, well, it's been, what, two hours since you dumped me, and you've already filled my place." A male voice. Marc assumed it was Lenny's.

"Maybe I should leave," Marc whispered, feeling the heat of passion vaporize like dry ice.

"So what's the little bastard have that I don't?" The voice was angry, slurred. And coming closer.

Penny turned to face Lenny, blocking his view of Marc. "First of all, I'm assuming you're drunk. And second, it's none of your damn business. Leave."

"No, no, Ms. Steale, you've always said that I'm a gentleman. And gentlemen introduce themselves, don't they?"

Marc whispered, "He's gonna find out sooner or later. Might as well be now." He stepped out behind Penny. "Ms. Steale asked you to leave. Please do so. Now." Marc's voice was lower and carried authority that he didn't feel he had the right to show, especially after their brief grope-fest.

In anticipation, Lenny had extended his right hand toward his contender. In the other hand he held a glass of wine. His hand stayed in the air for a few seconds as the race of his ex-fiancee's lover traveled from his eyes to his brain. Then the hand was extracted quickly, as if Marc could infect him with AIDS. "Dear God, Penny. Are you fucking Cowboy Troy?"

Penny turned to Marc. "Ignore him. Would you excuse us? It'll be just a minute."

Marc looked apprehensively at Lenny. "Okay. I'll be in …" He nodded toward the kitchen; Penny nodded back in assurance. She turned back to Lenny.

He just stood there. "Wow. I didn't figure you for a dark meat gal."

She wanted to say, "Don't be a dick," but instead she said, "Lenny, I hate to say this, but this has relatively little to do with you. I'll cut you some slack because it's been a rough day. But you cannot come in here and degrade my guest."

"Your 'guest'?" He smirked. "Jesus."

"Leave. Now. And give me your key, or I'll call security and tell them that you tried to assault me."

"Oh, I'm outta here," he said, handing over the key. "But remember. You said that I could tell the story. You know, the way I see it. And I see it quite differently now."

Marc came out of the kitchen in time to see him put the glass down and pick up a bag in one motion. Tipping an imaginary hat to the man who had just taken his woman away from him, he walked out the door.

Penny was quick to dead-bolt the lock, then walked over to the couch and crumbled.

Marc joined her. "God, I'm sorry, honey," he whispered as he held her.

"The little shit," she spurted. "Well, what else could happen?"

"Not much," Marc said, not knowing this was only the beginning of Penny's troubles. "This has been an intense time for you. Maybe I should go."

"No," she said. "I want you to stay. I'm not quite in the same space as I was when we came in, but I certainly can use some TLC. And I'm sorry about the 'dark meat' comment."

Marc shrugged. "Been called worse. Been called better, but been called worse."

* * * * * * * * * * *

Marc woke up when he heard the doorbell ring. And ring. Penny didn't stir. Without thinking, Marc unwound himself from Penny's sleepy embrace, got off the couch, grabbed a robe, and stumbled toward the offending noise.

He opened the door. A flash blinded him.

"Ms. Steale, would you comment—" Then the photographer looked at the face in the door and realized his mistake.

"I'm not Ms. Steale," Marc responded, not at all awake.

"Ah, better yet," he said, snapping another photo as he walked away.

"What's this about?" Marc demanded as the photographer ran toward the elevator.

"You can read all about it in the Monday edition. Sunday's already put to bed." He hopped on the elevator and waved as the doors closed.

* * * * * * * * * * *

When Marc woke the next morning, he shook off the last tendril of a dream, and promptly forgot it.

Penny woke with his stirring. "Mmmm," she said, squinting at the bright room. "You were restless last night. Did anyone ever tell you that you sleepwalk? You were doing it last night. I saw you headed for the bedroom. I just followed you in here. One-track mind, I guess." She traced the lace hem of the robe that Marc was wearing. Penny smiled. "It's you," she said, noting his choice of nightwear. "Peach is definitely your signature color."

"That's how we got in here," Marc replied, looking around the bedroom. They had been in the living room, that much he remembered. Then he caught the meaning of Penny's last statement. "What the—" he exclaimed, pulling off the frilly robe.

Twelve

"Pen, last night Lenny said something about taking you up on an offer. What was that about?" Marc asked as he read the Sunday issue of *Chicago Lives*. He wondered why Penny subscribed to this rag.

"What?" she said as she buttered, or more accurately, margarined, her toast. "Oh, about telling the story his way? Well, he had asked me if he could tell folks about the breakup. I agreed, because I knew he wanted to save his ego. What do I care how he tells it?"

"Well," Marc replied, handing over the paper, "he took you up on it. And I think you're going to care."

"'Another One Bites the Dust!'" she quoted from the title. "What the—listen to this!" She read it aloud, as if Marc hadn't seen it yet.

One more couple is added to the breakup list—this time, one of Chicago's very own.

Anyone who watched this year's Grammy Awards will recognize the names of Margo Steale and Lenny Blue. They were the Christian rockers who won the hearts of the audience and in homes across America and beyond—when Lenny, a funny, nervous man with Seinfeldian (or more accurately, Kramerian) timing—proposed to the lovely Margo Steale.

In front of millions of viewers, Lenny Blue, lead Chukka, got down on one knee and asked Ms. Steale to be his wife.

The audience went nuts. They got a standing ovation.

The viewers went nuts too. Their CD, *Steale Away*, doubled sales within one month after the telecast; last week *Steale Away* passed from gold to platinum. Those who purchased the album were not disappointed, as they found a refreshingly honest collection of songs about life, love, and occasionally, God.

And Lenny and Margo enjoyed a fairy-tale romance, almost naively tender, sailing on the sea of instant popularity and lucrative record sales. But it was not to be.

Lenny Blue noticed that his fiancée was becoming distant, almost cold to him. Ms. Steale began, well, stealing away after concerts, without explanation. But love was enough of a motivation for Lenny Blue to look the other way.

Until this weekend, when he waited for Ms. Steale in her apartment, intending to surprise her with a romantic evening. Except the surprise was on him. Imagine his shock upon finding his fiancée in the arms of another man.

"It's off," said a teary Lenny Blue. "I'm not sure how I will be able to get over this loss."

Ms. Steale was unavailable for comment.

"I can't even believe this," Penny said. "'Unavailable for comment.' How could I have been available? This went to press in the middle of the night. God, what was Lenny thinking? This has ruined any chance of our working together."

Marc was deep in thought.

"Marc?"

"Nothing," Marc said, unable to push his uneasiness aside. "Pen, he was drunk before he even saw you last night. I doubt that he was thinking about the long-term ramifications. What about you? How are you doing?"

"Just swell," she snipped. "Sorry. I don't need to take this out on anyone but Leonard." She tossed the paper aside.

Thirteen

Gary got to Penny's place as soon as he could.

"Penny, what's going on? Has Lenny finally melted down?" He turned his attention toward Marc. "And you must be the other man," he said, and they exchanged pleasantries. "Very nice to meet you." He was much more comfortable with all this than Marc would ever have imagined. Then again, Penny had said that they were best friends.

Penny disappeared for some reason or other. Gary sat down as if he was familiar with the place, which he was. "I'll be damned. Penny has been holding out on me. I've got to get that girl alone so we can talk about all this."

"Actually, 'all this' is quite a new thing," Marc said. "For one thing, I've only known Penny for two days. Time has certainly packed some interesting discoveries into these two days."

"I'm just grateful that someone knocked that jerk out of his orbit. You know, Lenny wasn't always like this. In the beginning there, we were good, uh, friends." His eyes wandered up toward the ceiling.

Marc caught his meaning immediately. "I'm assuming that you don't mean just drinking buddies. Does Penny know this?"

He sighed. “No. I was meaning to tell her Friday night. It was eating at me. I couldn’t let her go through with a sham of a marriage. Of course, I didn’t know that Penny wasn’t in love with him.”

“It didn’t seem like she had much time to discover that herself.”

“Hey, Marc, I would like to tell her about this, I mean, about me and Len. Okay?”

Marc nodded, just as Penny entered the room. Penny hugged Gary from behind. Then, pulling away, she said, “Gary, I’m sorry. Did I freak you out with this?” She placed herself between them on the couch.

“Yes. No. Well, yes, but in a good way,” Gary replied, trying to keep the smile out of his voice. “I think this is great.” He gave her hand a squeeze. “Kiddo, we need to talk,” he said into her sandy hair. “You owe me a conversation, remember?”

About a half hour later Penny and Gary returned from the bedroom. Gary continued his conversation. “And so after I called you, I went to the benefit down the street here and, well, I met someone. We’ll see how things go.”

Penny smiled and patted Gary’s tummy. “Back to the gym. Now I understand a little better about that muscle obsession. Or is it to boy-watch? Remind me to tell you about this dream I had yesterday.”

Gary smiled. “I’d better get going. Another date with Mr. Wonderful. I’ve got to get pretty.” He flashed a perfect smile; then his face got serious. “Just to warn you, there was already a crowd downstairs when I got here. I’d certainly use the Bat Cave,” he said, referring to Penny’s underground parking lot. “Are you going to be okay, kiddo?” His eyes were round with concern.

“Hey, I’m fine,” she lied. “Remember, I have to be tough to have a brother like Benji.”

Gary wasn’t satisfied, but he also knew when he needed to step aside. “Well, I’m off. Hey,” he said to Marc, “don’t let her get into any more trouble, okay?" Then he kissed Penny and flew out the door.

"So you know?" Marc asked.

"Did you?"

"Powers of deduction," Marc said cryptically. "Also known in certain communities as gaydar. It's an occupational hazard when hanging around a lesbian bar."

"God, a whole new vocabulary to learn." Penny smiled. "Which reminds me. We'll need to talk someday about your proclivities for lesbian drinking establishments."

Marc shrugged. "Yeah, well. I'm not sure if there is much logic to it." He laughed and rolled his eyes. "Another time. Why don't you start doing what you need to do? I'll just catch up on my TV watching." Marc had convinced her to stay at his apartment until the press got bored with the story. Penny immediately started her evacuation plan.

Marc could hear Penny on the phone, calling her neighbor to pick up her mail while she was gone. There were a few other housekeeping items she needed to take care of. And she still hadn't called her brother, so that was also on the to-do list before they left.

Marc thought about playing with Penny's computer but ended up spending forty minutes watching the closed-circuit view of the lobby, a security feature so that residents could buzz in their guests and not total strangers. Though the lobby was clear, Marc noticed a lot of activity outside the glass doors.

"Shall we?" Penny asked, bag in hand.

"Made all your calls?" There was only one that Marc was curious about. Her brother, Benjamin.

Penny knew that. "He wasn't home. I wish I knew where he was in all this."

Marc kissed her. "I don't think you should do this," she said, referring to Penny's plan to walk out of the building through the lobby. "Are you sure that you want to face the press? I mean, we can sneak you out."

Penny sighed. "I'm not looking forward to this. But I don't think that I will be able to avoid it forever, and I'd like to get the initial confrontation over with. There are certainly advantages in being in the public eye. I never thought much about the disadvantages. But you can't leave with me."

"Penny, I'm not leaving you alone with those vultures."

"You won't be—at least for that long. We talked about this. Right now, the issue is my breakup with Lenny, not you and me."

"The hell it's not," Marc said.

"Well, it shouldn't be," Penny said quietly. "I need to refocus the issue, and not let the media perpetuate their own fantasy." Not allowing further argument, Penny reviewed their plan. "You'll get the Jeep and wait. They're waiting for a show. Why not give them as little as possible?"

Marc knew this was a bad idea. He even begged Penny to talk with her friend Daniel, the lawyer. But Marc already knew enough about Penny to know when to stop beating his head against a wall. "At least don't wear that red jacket. It screams Scarlett O'Hara."

"Couldn't if I wanted to," Penny said. "I must have left it at your place. But I am wearing my boots." She kissed Marc and sent him out the door with her set of keys and a medium-sized bag. Marc took the luggage to the elevator and, using Penny's special passkey, descended to the underground parking lot where he had parked the night before. Marc loaded the Jeep with a heaviness he could not blame on Penny's luggage.

Marc agreed with Penny when she spoke of the advantages and disadvantages of being in the public eye. But it was more than just taking the bad with the good. In Marc's experience, he found the press sometimes walked a sloppy line between reporting the news and exploiting the victims. Marc had experienced this reality all too early in his life.

It didn't make national news, the crash of Sky Window Flight 1081, but it did rearrange the universe for Marc and Spooner, who was known as Clarissa at that point in her life. Their mother had died during that crash. He could still remember those reporters, lined outside their grandparents' door, waiting to see the tears of two little kids.

"Sick bastards," he said, indicting both the past and the present media.

Marc pulled himself behind the steering wheel and put the car into motion. As directed, he waited in the fire lane outside the building. *Or was it the firing line?* he wondered.

The crowd had swallowed Penny up. Marc tracked her as she moved in and out of view. "Come on, come on, let her through," he said, feeling a knot in his stomach. Finally, Penny pulled on the door handle and jumped in.

"Vultures," Marc muttered as he pulled away from the curb. "Are you okay?"

"Actually, I'm a mess, but it wasn't as bad as I thought. Though I now know why I couldn't get Benjamin. He was here, waiting for me. Always working the crowd. Look," she said, pointing, "he's the fat one. Look's like they're getting some copy from him too. He always had to have the last word."

Marc looked at her. "You mean, he was here waiting for you instead of talking with you privately? That's sick. Sorry; I shouldn't have said that. I mean, he is your brother." He drove them down Michigan Avenue north toward Lake Shore Drive and into the anonymity of traffic.

"They didn't know who he was until he opened his mouth. 'Sis,' he says, 'what you're doing is wrong. Come back to Jesus. We'll get you help.' How sincere. Of course, he could have called me and said the same thing without the aid of the press. And I'm not sure what's so wrong." She sat back in the seat. "Damn," she exhaled, hitting her forehead, "I've completely forgotten about my folks. I don't want them to hear this on the news." Sigh. "Remind me to do that when we get home. I mean, to your place."

Marc pulled out his cell phone. "Want to call them now?"

Penny shook her head quickly. "Thanks, but I have mine." She pulled out the phone but let it drop back into her purse. "I don't know what to say. I'll have to think it over."

They passed high-rise buildings on their left and the peaceful harbors dotting Lake Michigan on their right. It was still too early for most of the pleasure boats to be docked, though an occasional tour yacht hugged the coast. After twenty minutes of mostly silent motoring during which Marc watched Penny glance over her shoulder too many times, he merged right to exit.

"I think someone is following us," Penny said.

"I know. The sedan. Damn press," Marc muttered. As they exited on Foster Avenue, he made a quick call. They continued to Lincoln Avenue, and he pulled over by the police precinct. The car following them quickly turned into the shopping plaza across the street.

A woman came over to Marc's window with the familiarity of a friend. "Hello, Hawthorne. Is that the guy over there?" The woman nodded at the car in question.

"Yep," Marc answered. "This is Penny Lane."

"A.k.a. Margo Steale," Boots said, nodding at her. "You're certainly quite popular these days."

Penny groaned. "A little too much, if you get my drift."

Boots turned toward the car. "You know I can't do much," she said to Marc.

"Just scare the hell out of him. Tell him that I'm considering pressing charges for stalking."

"Are you?" Boots inquired.

"Yes, if that's what you need to hear."

"Okay, Hawthorne. Even if he does comply, you should file a complaint. And you know that I can't legally do a thing to him." She referred to her status as an ex-member of the Chicago Police Department.

"Yes, okay. Just get him out of here."

Boots gave them a somber look, then turned away.

Penny watched Boots walk over to the car that had trailed them since downtown. "Boots, huh? She's quite an attractive woman. Native American?"

"Yeah. Lakota. She's a good, uh, friend." This was beginning to sound like a code. "Friend" equals "ex-lover."

"An ex?"

"Well, yes, years ago. It was relatively brief. I wasn't very mature. I certainly didn't understand our cultural differences." Marc was getting uncomfortable. "Pen, I haven't had that many relationships in my thirty-some years. Unfortunately, some of them end up as friends. Is that weird for you?"

Penny took a closer look at Marc's ex-girlfriend. Boots was a tall woman, with pleasing curves and a softness not obscured by her jeans and denim shirt. "Are you still in touch with the others? Your other ex-lovers?"

"Not really. I had a fling in grad school, but she is in Montana with her wilderness husband. There's Dale, a therapist that I see around town once in a while. Boots. Other than that, my work has kept me pretty unattached."

As Marc finished his sentence, they watched the guy pull away. Boots came back. "I recognized this one. He's a particularly pesky one. I'll check on you tonight, Hawthorne. Will you be home?"

"Of course," Marc said. "Thanks."

"Hold on," Boots ordered. "I wouldn't be surprised if he keeps following you. Keep going north, then double back in a few miles. I'll stay here you until you pass the station. If you're clear, sail on. If not, I'll have one of the boys get him."

They thanked her again and pulled out. Penny was quiet.

"What are you thinking about?" Marc asked.

"Oh, nothing," she said. "Just how weird life can be sometimes. It seems as if life has spun out of control since those damn Grammys. Not that I'm not grateful to be able to do what I love. It's the other stuff."

Marc understood a bit of Penny's dilemma. This was why he had vetoed 80 percent of his publicist's ideas. He didn't need to be the new science poster child, even if it meant more book sales. He'd rather hang out with his elementary school kids looking at the stars.

"You know?" Penny's question broke through his recollection. Marc wasn't sure what she was asking assent to. "Sorry?"

"Earth to Dr. Hubble."

So she knows about my work with the Hubble too, thought Marc.

"What else did you find out about me, besides the Hubble?" Marc wanted to know.

"You were all over the news with that Pathfinder stuff years ago, and recently when we blew up the moon. Other NASA stuff. Pretty impressive. And you're the March feature on the 'Young Scientists' home page."

"You get an A-minus for your homework, Penny."

"Just an A-minus?" she asked.

"If you had found the scandalous references, then you might have gotten an A. But there will be plenty of time for that later."

They followed Boots's directives. They drove past the station. No sign of the car. Boots waved them on. A few minutes later, they pulled into the parking lot without incident.

Fourteen

Boots came over much later that night. "Is Ms. Steale here?" she asked.

"No. She went to talk with her brother. This whole thing is turning out to be a circus." Marc waved Boots inside.

"That ain't the half of it," Boots said as she plopped on the sofa. "Mind if I smoke?"

"Now what's going on?" Marc asked, knowing Boots only smoked if something was wrong.

Boots lit up, then sank back into the couch. "An hour ago I heard a call come in from a buddy of mine on the South Side. It seems like your friend's ex-fiancé just offed himself."

"Offed himself? Lenny Blue? You mean, he committed suicide?"

"Well, that's how it's being reported on TV. There's an investigation going on right now."

"When did this happen?"

"Don't know." Boots looked Marc squarely in the eye. "How long has Steale been gone?"

Marc hesitated.

"Marc," she said, unaware that she only had addressed Marc by his first name while they were lovers, "I'm not even on the force anymore, so I'm not here as a cop. I do have to warn you, though. There will be an investigation if all the pieces don't fit. Steale will be called in for the standard series of questions, just like the others. It will all come out."

"Boots, she didn't kill her ex."

"She probably didn't. But things are going to heat up a bit for her."

"What do you suggest we should do?"

Boots's first thought was to tell her previous lover to keep the hell out of it. But she knew Marc was already involved over his head and wouldn't hear her. Instead Boots advised him: "Find her a good lawyer. See if D2 is anywhere around. And stop her from making any more public statements." She looked around for somewhere to put out her cigarette. Marc took it from her. "Hawthorne, I've got to go. Get a lawyer tonight. And don't let Steale disappear."

Boots left. Like Spooner, she was never one to linger.

Marc took the last few puffs on Boots's cigarette as he flicked on the news. He turned to channel 3 and within minutes caught the whole story, or as whole as they were presenting it. Marc's least favorite reporter, Leslie Quipley, was stationed outside a small house in a residential neighborhood.

Leslie looked intensely at the camera as she began her report. "Earlier this weekend we learned that Margo Steale and Lenny Blue, popular musicians from the religious music scene, were terminating their engagement because of Ms. Steale's alleged affair," she intoned in a serious voice. "We caught up with Ms. Steale outside her posh Michigan Avenue condo earlier this afternoon."

The camera cut to Penny's statement just a few hours earlier, clipped to sound bite–sized proportions. "I am sorry that Mr. Blue needed to communicate his grief over our breakup in the way he did. I regret that he twisted the events to portray himself as the victim." She was eloquent. She was beautiful.

But Penny's words also portrayed her as cold, exacting. The station edited out any footage of emotion they could. She was being painted as an unfeeling bitch living in the lap of luxury.

The reporter blabbed on over the taped footage. "Ms. Steale's manager, who is also her brother, was also available for comment."

This was the first good look Marc got at Benjamin. He was a handsome man, physically similar to Penny, but was carrying about seventy-five pounds of excess weight. Even so, with his well-made suit and conservatively cut hair, he was able to pull off a look of rational concern. Until he opened his mouth.

Benjamin Lane had scanned the crowd, then zeroed in on the camera with the subtlety of a heat-seeking missile. "Margo, Margo," he started with a disconcerting parental voice. "We love you. We want you to come back. You know what I mean. 'Home' to the Lord." He drew quotations around the word "home," then wiped away what appeared to Marc as a manufactured tear. "She wasn't always like this, folks," he explained to the television audience. "Satan can deceive anyone who gives him a foothold."

Marc could not believe that any network would broadcast this shit. And he couldn't believe that these two were siblings.

He also was confused as to why Benjamin thought his sister had been possessed by Satan. What was going on in his mind that he would jump to that conclusion?

Quipley continued from outside Lenny's apartment. "The story turned a tragic corner this evening, when police found Mr. Blue dead in his South Side apartment. I'm standing outside his home. Though the police have not issued an official statement, our sources are calling it a suicide at his own hands."

"Of course, a suicide at someone else's hand would not be a suicide," Marc muttered to himself. "Twit."

Then the camera cut back to the anchor of the station, George Sweet. "Leslie, is there any word from the relatives, or from Ms. Steale?"

The camera cut back to Quipley. "George, the parents have already identified the body, and it has been taken away—"

"Must have gotten there too late for that little scene. What a great little morsel that would have been." Marc's voice was acid.

"—but no statement has been, uh, collected from Ms. Steale since her ex-fiancé's death."

"Thank God for small miracles," Marc sighed. But where was Ms. Steale? He clicked off the TV just as they were announcing the night's winning lottery numbers.

Penny was in a no-win situation. Even if they did find it a suicide, the press had already tried and convicted her of a crime more heinous than one of passion. One of passionlessness.

Fifteen

The phone jarred Marc awake. "Yeah?" he asked, stiff from the unnatural sleeping position he found himself in for the third night in a row. He really needed to stop sleeping on the couch.

"Turn on channel three. I'll be right over," Spooner said.

Marc looked at the clock—2:17 AM. Where the hell was Penny? He flipped on the set. It was a rebroadcast of the ten o'clock news. Marc watched the last part of Leslie Quipley's report. Spooner must have just closed down the bar, gone home, turned on the TV, and seen this.

Then Marc noticed a pair of red boots by the door. He looked in the bedroom. Penny must have gone right into bed without waking him. She was sound asleep.

Marc rang Spooner back and caught her just as she was walking out the door. "Let's meet at the bar."

Silence. Then, "She's there, isn't she?"

"Give me two minutes," Marc said as he considered wearing the boots but instead wiggled into his battered running shoes. "I'll be right there."

Spooner was waiting. The alarm system was disengaged. Only the security lights were on. The jukebox glowed too brightly in the dimness. Marc was still not quite awake, and barely noticed the messy counter and tables.

"Was that your Jeep?" Spooner asked.

What was she talking about? Marc wondered.

"Your Jeep. On the news, there was a black guy in a green Jeep." She exhaled. "Are you involved in this mess?"

"Oh, come on. I drove Penny from her apartment. Is that now a crime?"

"Boots was in. She's a little concerned about your friend. And about you." Spooner stayed behind the counter. Her power position.

"Great," Marc quipped. "A united front."

"I think we have the right to worry about you. Look at you. You've known this girl for, what, two days? Within those two days, she has been the focus of a sex scandal, namely with you, and a suspect in a murder investigation."

"A sex scandal? Spooner, did you really say that? Now who's the prude?"

Spooner ignored Marc and poured a shot of bourbon as she continued. "I hate to tell you this, but that is not a normal sequence for a romance. Usually people have a lot of sex, drop out of the public eye, and then wake up a day, or a week, or maybe a month later to find that the world has gone on without them. They usually don't *televise it*!" The last words grew considerably louder than the first. She downed the bourbon in one gulp.

"What do you think this is about?" Marc asked. "It's not like she said, 'Hey, Marc, you are such a great lover that I am going to kill my ex, just so there is no question in his mind or yours.' And this is not a murder investigation. It's a suicide."

"Have it your way," she said.

Marc walked away, ready to go out the door, and then turned around. He couldn't leave it like this between them. "Pour me a shot."

She did. They drank in silence.

Spooner broke the quiet. "Hey, kid, I'm sorry. Maybe I was stupid and overreacted. But you have to admit that you've kinda been stupid too. Not that love won't drive you to do stupid things. Though this has to be the stupidest thing you've ever done."

"What if it's not?" Marc asked, not completely convinced that Spooner was wrong this time. "If it's not the stupidest thing, what then?"

"You are in love with her, aren't you?"

Marc felt his face get warmer. Damn alcohol. Rolling his eyes, he confessed, "Yeah, I am. And though I hate to say you were right, I guess I fell for her when she walked through that door."

Spooner set down her glass firmly. "Damn. If you're not just being stupid, and she doesn't end up fucking things up, then you're probably the luckiest guy alive."

"Luck be a lady tonight," Marc said, raising his glass. "Maybe it'll be my new song."

"Just get her a lawyer, okay?" she said as she walked away. "And turn on the damn alarm of yours on when you leave. By the way," she added. "You're not the only one who has a woman waiting in your bed." She smiled weakly and then walked out the door.

Sixteen

"I tried to wake you, but you wouldn't move," Penny said sleepily when Marc crawled into bed next to her.

"I wish I weren't awake now." Marc leaned against the headrest. He could still taste the bourbon on his tongue.

Now Penny was awake. "Was someone here earlier? I smelled cigarette smoke. What's up?"

First things first, thought Marc. "Did you connect with Benjamin?"

"No. I tried him at his place, but he wasn't home. So I just drove around for a while."

"For six hours?"

"Marc, what's going on? Did they broadcast that stuff outside my apartment again?"

No use in even trying to sleep. Marc leaned over and turned on the lamp. "Oh, Penny, it's worse than that. Lenny's dead."

Penny stared. "What? No. Dead?" The words were making no sense.

Marc took her hand. "They think it's a suicide, but Boots is suggesting that the police will be conducting some type of investigation. Where you've been the last six hours will be very important to them, especially if they suspect that it was murder and not a suicide."

"Lenny's dead? You'd better start from there."

Marc told her how Boots had come over, and about the broadcast. "Boots suggested that you get a lawyer, and don't give any more statements to the press."

"I guess I can call my lawyer," she said. "Although my lawyer is—was also Lenny's."

"Not a good idea."

"Yes, you're right," Penny said, distant in thought.

"Listen, I do have a friend who is a lawyer. He works for a firm downtown, actually not too far away from your condo. He's the one person I could call in the middle of the night who would come here."

"A lawyer. Maybe this is unnecessary. In the middle of the night?" Penny's voice tightened. "I can't believe this. I'm just …" Her voice trailed off in grief.

With a graceful economy of movement, Marc leaned over to pick up the phone and pulled Penny closer to him. "This has gotten a bit larger than a reputation problem, Pen. If they find something suspicious, I want you to be covered. I think it is being wise about the realties." Marc dialed the phone. After a weak hello from whom he assumed to be Daniel on the other end, he said, "Hey, it's Marcus."

"Welby, I hope." He slurred his words sleepily.

"No, the other one," Marc said seriously.

"Isn't this a bit compulsive?" Daniel asked. "I told you that your taxes would be done before April fifteenth. You know that I'm not a tax lawyer. Nor am I an accountant. My clock says it's 3:48. Why in hell would you be calling now?"

"I need you to come over. We'll talk when you get here."

"It better be a good one, Hawthorne. Even Marcus Welby couldn't get a rise out of me this early, and you know how I like doctors."

Daniel only lived ten minutes away, so he arrived only moments after the coffee stopped brewing. "Marc," he said, still hazy from sleep, "I know that I owed you one, but this better be good."

"Daniel Weaver, this is Penny Lane," Marc said. "Penny, Dan. Penny's the reason I called you. I made coffee."

Daniel was a boyishly handsome man who seemed to have just recently grown into his over-six-foot body. He was trim with pale blond hair, penetrating gray eyes, and dimples. A slight growth of stubble dotted his strong chin. "Oh my God, it's Margo Steale," he said, recognizing Penny immediately. "We'll, you have been keeping the news busy in the last few days." His response rang similar to Boots's comments earlier that day.

"Great," Penny said, collapsing on the couch, "I've become notorious."

He laughed, a hearty laugh that almost made both of them smile. "Not quite Billy the Kid status yet. If the truth be told, however, I"—his voice dropped to a whisper—"I was one of those saps who bought your CD after the Grammys. I guess you don't have to be straight to be a sucker for romance. It's actually one of my favorites."

Marc went to get the coffee. "D2, I'm sorry I was so cryptic on the phone, but I thought that it would be better for Penny to tell you about all this."

"That's fine. I probably wouldn't have understood it anyway. Penny, I did read the *Chicago Lives* blurb and saw your statement outside your 'posh Michigan Avenue condo.' Wait, Marc," he asked as he reappeared in the room, "was that you in that Jeep?"

"Yes." Marc had a feeling that this was going to be a popular question.

"So, you two are—together?" Daniel said. "God, this is much better than the Grammys. Congratulations!" He sat back on the couch. "Marc, I can't believe this! Wow. I mean, don't you just love her stuff?"

Marc bit his lip. "I—really haven't had time to research—"

Dan was hysterical. "You're dating a Grammy, and you don't know a damn thing about her music?" He turned to Penny. "I suppose you don't know that he has a book. *Once Upon a Universe.* Currently on the *New York Times* bestsellers list."

"Really?" Penny responded, wondering how she had missed that piece of information from her Internet research the day before.

"It's not really that big of a deal," Marc said. Penny could tell that Marc was lying. "In comparison with everything that has gone on in the last few days, it's small potatoes. It's really a science geek book."

"Penny," Daniel said, "it is definitely not a geek book. He's been proclaimed as the next Sagan or Hawking, but better looking." He shot a look at Marc.

"D2, I'm not sure that either one would appreciate the comparison," Marc said, wishing that they could get on with business.

Daniel recognized his friend's impatience. "Okay, back to the subject. Frankly, I don't think I'm going to be much help. I'd imagine that you're interested in dissolving a partnership with Mr. Blue. In that case, you may want to contact lawyers who specialize in this stuff."

Penny looked at Marc, puzzled.

Marc read her mind. "You didn't catch the ten o'clock reports, did you, D2? Lenny Blue is dead. They are saying that it's a suicide, but Boots is suggesting that it could blow open into something larger."

The atmosphere cooled dramatically. "Oh, God," Daniel said. "I am really sorry. I had no idea, otherwise I wouldn't have been so flip. I didn't hear about any of this. Of course, this changes the situation completely. Whether this is fortunate or unfortunate for you, this puts this case squarely into my line of expertise." He settled into the chair. "You'd better play it from the beginning. And I mean the beginning."

Penny summarized the last few months of her relationship with Lenny Blue, coming all the way to the activities of Friday night: how she left the concert at the encore, ending up at Spooner's and meeting Marc. Then she got reticent and looked at Marc for guidance.

"He already knows we're together," Marc said, giving her permission.

"Penny," Daniel said, "you certainly don't have to go into details with the police, but I do need to know where you were during this time. For now, it's enough to know that you were here. We'll decide together how much detail the police need to know after that."

Marc took over. "D2, Penny spent the night here Friday night and tonight—Sunday night. I was at her place Saturday night."

"Well," Penny corrected, "I wasn't here all last night. We came back here yesterday afternoon at about, what time, Marc, five?"

"Yeah, about that. We flipped through the local news stations. Some had covered Penny outside the condo. Others hadn't. They always stagger the news around the five-to-six hour, so five sounds right."

"Then," Penny continued, "I took Marc's Jeep and tried to go talk with my brother up at his house in Rogers Park. I was furious about his 'come to Jesus' plea for me on the network, and wanted to set things straight. Anyway, he wasn't there. Then I realized that he was probably at church." Then she stopped again.

"Well, go ahead," he prodded.

"Benjamin is on staff at Family First Church down by Lincoln Park. That's where we had the concert the other night. Anyway, I found his car and parked next to it, thinking that he had to come out eventually. I waited for about a half hour, but I got impatient. I decided to go in. And there he was, at the podium, preaching up a storm. Before I had a chance to take a seat, he spotted me. You can imagine what the topic changed to, but at least he didn't publicly humiliate me like he did earlier in the day. I discreetly gave him the finger, and then left. Not without writing him a nasty note and putting it under his windshield wiper. That was about eight or so. Then I just drove down Lake Shore Drive and back up."

"You didn't go to Lenny's place, did you?" he asked.

"Well, that was my original intention. But I was so distracted that I ended up getting lost in Hyde Park. I guess I wasn't in the right mind set to deal with him anyway. So I turned around and came back. When I got here, Marc was asleep on the couch. I tried to wake him, but he wouldn't budge. That was about eleven thirty."

"You didn't tell me about the church thing," Marc said, trying not to sound defensive.

Penny looked at him. "I didn't have a chance."

Daniel got out of the chair. "Penny, we've got some work to do. You have a large hole in your alibi, and it sounds like it's at exactly the wrong time. This is not saying that you did anything wrong," he added, waving his hands. "We just have to make sure no one tries to fill in the blank for us." He stopped, massaging his forehead.

"Aspirin?" Marc asked.

"No, I was just thinking. It's too bad that Benny didn't identify you at the church. At least that would anchor your story and your location on the North Side. Do you know if anyone else saw you or recognized you?"

"Daniel, I have no idea. People could have been pointing and staring, but I was so angry at Ben that I was only paying attention to him."

"Can we go back a bit? What happened between Friday night and tonight?"

Penny filled in the details that she had missed. Saturday afternoon's conversation with Lenny, when Penny broke up with him. Lenny's discovery of Penny and Marc. Gary's visit. Then the dash from Penny's condo.

Dan asked, "Have you talked with your friend Gary since Lenny's death?"

"No," Penny said. "I didn't know myself until Marc came back from Spooner's."

"Besides," Marc added, "I think he was on a date with someone he met at the benefit. Hey, how was that?" he asked Daniel.

Dan was momentarily confused. "Uh, yeah. Again, thanks for the tickets. You're right about those things. It was mostly boring, but I did make a business connection there. What's this about Spooner?" he asked Marc.

"Spooner called me up after she closed the bar to grill me about my involvement. She saw me in the Jeep, too, and was worried. Typical Spooner stuff."

"Well," he said, standing up, "we do need to have a plan. I want to see both of you in my office tomorrow morning—I mean, later this morning. Both of you, take a cab."

"I really can't use the Jeep?"

"No. A cab," he said. "Now, this all sounds cloak-and-dagger, but there is a reason. The whole world knows where Penny lives. I don't want everyone to know who Marc is or where he lives. If there is a way that you can garage the Jeep, until this is over—"

"D2, I need a car!"

"Then rent one. Something understated, like a Cobalt," he added. "And Marc, you know that Penny can't stay here."

"Oh, come on," Marc said.

"It's for the good of both of you. It will not help Penny if you are dragged into this. It will reinforce the media's perception that Penny is entrenched with a new lover while her old one is barely dead."

"Lenny and I were never really lovers," Penny said. "I mean, in the true sense of the word. And technically," she added, "Marc and I have never …" Her voice trailed off.

Marc shrugged and looked at Daniel. "What can I say? Inconvenient things keep happening."

"They don't know that," he said. "Very little of this is about reality. We need to give them as little material as possible. I hate to say this, but I want the two of you to stay out of the public eye for a while. I'd say to avoid being together, but first of all, that's cruel, and second of all, you wouldn't listen to me anyway. Please be discreet. Don't let anyone into your apartment unless you know them. And only if you know them well."

"This feels very weird to me," Penny said. "I mean, Lenny is dead, and I am plotting my defense." The reality hit again. "I mean, Lenny's dead."

Marc put his arms around her. "I'm sorry. You haven't even had time to process this."

Penny's tears came fast. "I didn't mean for this to happen." Emotion broke her speech. "I just didn't want to marry him. I still loved him as a friend."

Marc stiffened. Something was odd about what she said. He looked at Dan; he had caught it too. Why did her words sound like a confession?

Daniel stared at Marc. "I think we're done for now. Marc, I want to see you in my office at nine AM. You can come back and help Penny pack. Penny, why don't you come around noon?"

Before he completely slid out the door, he added one more instruction: "No statements to the press or to the police. From either one of you. Not unless I'm there." The door shut, then reopened. "And lock this door."

Marc held Penny as the recognition of reality settled around her. But what exactly was Penny grieving?

Seventeen

Daniel stripped off the sweat suit he had worn over to Marc's and got back into bed. A glance at the clock told him that it was almost six. "Shit," he exhaled. Why bother trying to get back to sleep when he had to get up in an hour?

"Hey, lover boy, who's Marcus Welby? Should I be jealous?" Strong arms pulled him close.

"Watch it there!" Daniel said as his bedmate reached inside his shorts. Normally Daniel would have entertained this proposition, but for once something else overrode his desire. "I have to ask you something. You're probably going to think I'm weird for asking this, but you wouldn't happen to be a friend of Margo Steale, would you?"

Daniel felt Gary's grip loosen; then a hand withdrew from Daniel's BVDs. "How did you know that?" Gary asked, looking at him with bewildered eyes.

Daniel realized that not only was he in a delicate situation—one that could compromise his newest client—but he was now also an alibi.

"Cowboy," Daniel said, "we've got a lot of talking to do."

Eighteen

"This is no simple suicide," Boots told Spooner. "I can feel it."

"Shit," Spooner replied as she rolled over. Propping her head in one hand, she took a long draw off her cigarette, apparently not at all aware of how sexy she looked to Boots.

Boots tried to keep her eyes on Spooner's face. "Did Hawthorne hear you? About the lawyer?" Boots found her glance tracing Spooner's shapely body. So much for discipline.

Spooner was distracted. "I think so. He's so damned sure of himself. But I'm sure I'm not telling you anything you don't already know."

That was true. They both knew a lot about Hawthorne, Boots mused. "The kid is really over his head with this one. I could tell when I talked with him earlier this evening." Boots was still a bit unsure as to how this current scenario had occurred. She hoped she wasn't using Spooner as a substitute for her brother in some weird, sexual way.

Spooner, on the other hand, didn't seem at all bothered with bedding her brother's ex-girlfriend.

"He had fooled himself into thinking that he is the most objective person when it comes to this shit. He's just as fucking irrational about love as everyone else—probably worse, with all that star shit in his eyes. He is way past head over heels. Oh well," Spooner said, shaking her head. "Enough of this Marc talk. How about us?" she whispered as she sidled her naked body up to Boots. "Why hadn't we thought of this before?"

"Good question," Boots replied as she rolled on top of her and kissed her deeply, though deep down Boots suspected the answer could be found in two words.

Marcus Hawthorne.

* * * * * * * * * *

At 4:24 AM, after kissing a sleeping Spooner on the cheek, Boots rolled out of bed, into her off-duty clothes (all her clothes were now off-duty clothes), and left the apartment. Although she wasn't due at the station until, well, ever, she wanted to find out what she could about the death of Lenny Blue. She didn't want to think too much about why she had left the bed of a beautiful woman.

This Lenny Blue thing nagged at her. Boots knew it was too early for an official ruling. Suicide was more likely dreamed up by the press in the wake of a deadline. What she had heard last night on the police bands was not clear, but it suggested a different story. Most of the time, she didn't have access to an investigation as she did when she was a cop. Fortunately, the death took place in a precinct where she had a good connection.

Boots jumped into her sedan. She chose a route that took her past Marc's loft and noticed the lights on.

Unlike during rush hour, Lake Shore Drive at 4:50 AM was a breeze. Even so, a number of people were on their way to work or only now going home after pulling a graveyard shift. She reached the Fifty-Third-Street exit within twenty-five minutes.

Lenny Blue had lived on one of the nonparallel, serpentine streets that lay between Fifty-Third and Hyde Park Boulevard. Being unfamiliar with this part of Hyde Park, she would have passed the house altogether if the front yard hadn't been knotted with yellow "do not cross" tape. Two unmarked cars were double parked. She followed their example as she rolled to a stop behind them. Her car blended right in.

James Bay stood in the doorway. "Jimmy." She extended her hand to her old friend. Jimmy had been her first and only partner on the force. He had been transferred to a South Side precinct after the incident responsible for terminating her job as a cop. "Who's here?" she asked, referring to the presence of the second car.

He shook her hand. "Good to see you, Boots." Jimmy's smile crinkled his craggy Irish face, making him look older than his age of forty-something. He ran a hand through short but thick dark hair. He was a few inches shy of six feet. "Most of them left at about two. As you can see, there isn't much to check. The kid had very little."

That was an understatement, Boots thought as she walked into the one-room apartment. A futon couch lined one wall. The other objects were less recognizable under the dust. A guitar leaned against one wall, plugged into what looked like an amplifier the size of a dishwasher. A bookshelf, with titles hidden by fingerprint dust, and what Boots guessed to be a stereo unit opposite the couch. And on the fourth wall, a dinette set, vintage Ward and June Cleaver. Quite a different lifestyle than the one allegedly lived by Ms. Steale.

A crimson shadow of the body was marked in blood on the floor by the dinette set. It looked as if Lenny's last moments were spent sitting at the table before he collapsed onto the floor. Much of the blood on the table had been covered by the fingerprint dust, creating a thick, tarry paste. Boots recognized the pattern of the gray Formica through a large clean square in the center of the table. It would match the tables at Jimmy's favorite greasy spoon on the North Side of the city. She looked at the precision of edge of the square, and decided that whatever had been on the table was already bagged for evidence.

"This is the whole thing," Jimmy said, waving an arm around him. "It's a studio. He used his parents' kitchen and bathroom."

"The parents live upstairs?" she asked. "So they discovered the body?"

"Yeah. I questioned the parents and the neighbors. There's some discrepancy about their discovery and the time of death—"

Jimmy stopped as another detective stepped through the door. "Uh," he said, "Sandra Rudd, this is John Bryson. Bryson is supervising the investigation."

"Detective Bryson," Boots said, shaking his hand. He had a rigid grip, like a vice. He was a white man with perfect teeth but otherwise an unremarkable face. He stood slightly over six feet tall.

"Early shift?" Bryson asked.

"No, PI," she replied honestly.

Bryson looked at Boots suspiciously, then turned to Jimmy, who gave a barely perceptible nod. "So you're Boots. Bay's talked a hell of a lot about you, that you've pulled his chestnuts from the fire a good number of times." He paused. "Oh, hell. Maybe you can help us out with this one. Whatcha want to know?"

Boots recognized the "chestnut" expression as vintage Jimmy. She was grateful he had paved the way for her. Since some cops tended to be too territorial for their own good, Boots found Bryson's invitation refreshing. "So what's the parents' story?"

"Well, it's a little strange," Jimmy interjected, not wanting to be left out. "Apparently they had just rented an old Jean-Claude Van Damme movie. Their volume was up so high that they didn't hear a thing. One of the neighbors heard gunshots and called them up. The father answered the phone, insisted that she was hearing the movie, and promised to turn it down, which they did. Then the neighbor calls back, asks why she had only heard gunshots and nothing else from the movie."

"You mean, like no voices or music?" Boots probed.

"Yeah, like that. They turned the sound down, but there's no more shooting. But a few moments later, when they heard something downstairs, they investigated. That's when they found him—about nine. They're both emotionally wrecked. The press being here within twenty minutes didn't help much."

"Great," she said, amazed at the speed of the media.

Jimmy added, "Well, the press was helped along this time. Leslie Quipley is a neighbor. She found out right away and once Channel 3 was here, then everyone was. We barely got the body out."

Boots groaned. That meant they rushed.

"Don't worry," Bryson said, answering her unspoken thought, "Dr. Bridge is also a neighbor and family friend, and she was able to examine the body before we moved him anywhere." Catherine Bridge was a medical examiner Boots had watched perform dozens of autopsies at the county morgue.

"About the neighbor who called, how many gunshots did she hear?" Boots asked.

"Two," said Jimmy.

"Did they find two bullets?"

"Yep," Bryson replied. "Obviously the first one missed the target. Shot out the amp over there. The other one, well, it hit the mark," he said, his arm sweeping the bloodied room.

"Was the gun recovered?"

Bryson nodded. "Smith and Wesson .38."

Boots groaned again. It was a common handgun, and unless it was registered, it would likely be untraceable. "Prints on the gun?"

Bryson shrugged. "Some partials. We'll know after they run them."

Boots looked around the room. "Jimmy, you said something about a noise. I'm assuming that they didn't hear a gunshot. How long after the shots did the parents hear the noise down here?"

"They figured no more than maybe a minute after the neighbor called. And the neighbor called right after they heard the shots."

"So, any thoughts about the noise? The body dropping off the chair? Someone helping his body off the chair?" The latter theory would suggest homicide.

Bryson scratched the back of his neck. "I'd bet the latter. Especially given the fact that Lenny Blue didn't die here."

"What? The body was moved here?" Boots then remembered what Jimmy had begun to tell her right before she met Bryson. "Jimmy, is this what you were talking about? This time differential between the death and the parents' discovery?"

Bryson spoke. "The autopsy will be the definitive word, but ME's guessing that the death was at least a couple hours before discovery. Prelims say it could be as much as eight." He shrugged again.

"Wow," Boots said, startled by this revelation. This changed the scenery completely. "So we're possibly looking at two crime scenes?"

"That's what I was starting to tell you earlier," Jimmy said. "Lividity places Blue in a different position than he could have been in, either at the table here or on the floor the way he was found." He pointed at the marks on the floor. "Here's the head," he said, pointing to the place where a lot of blood had spattered and pooled. "As you can probably tell from the splatter marks, Blue supposedly shot himself in the head while propped at the table. First, why would it take two shots for him to find his head?" Then he pointed at the walls, which recorded red arcs away from where they estimated Blue's head had been. "And second, rigor doesn't back up the scenario. Because rigor had not completely done its thing, Blue's hand was manipulated to look as if he pulled the trigger while reading the *Chicago Lives* article about his failed love relationship. We actually found the body with his right hand index finger caught behind the trigger. I'm not sure how he could have pulled the trigger like that. Blue then fell from an upright sitting position to the floor onto his right side—"

"Or more accurately, he was helped onto the floor," Bryson corrected.

Jimmy proceeded as if Bryson hadn't interrupted him. "Like I said, he falls onto his right side. Lividity indicates that he died on his left side, or that he fell on his left side after his death."

"So the gun is a worthless prop all around." Bryson exhaled. "Much ado about nothing."

Boots understood Bryson's frustration. Ultimately, if Blue died before the shooting, the real death had nothing to do with the gun. And since the shooter left the gun behind, it was probably stolen or unregistered. It was a prop. Perhaps not worthless, but not very helpful at this point in the investigation. She had been right. This was no simple suicide.

"Anything else recovered?" she asked.

"I imagine you've been following the story about Margo Steale and her breakup with the victim." Bryson shook his head. "Stupid question. Who's been able to avoid it?" He looked at the spot on the table Boots had observed earlier. "We found two things. Like he said, *Chicago Lives* was sitting on the table, as if he was reading the article about his breakup with Ms. Steale. So, how would you call it?"

It was Boots's turn to shrug. "First, that someone thought we would be fooled by the suicide thing—that Lenny Blue killed himself because of his breakup with Margo Steale. Or second, that someone wanted to frame Margo Steale."

"A logical guess," Bryson maintained. "The second thing wasn't in the apartment. It was in a Dumpster just behind the house, buried under trash and some old curtains. A red leather jacket. With a helluva lot of blood on it. I'm guessing that it's Lenny Blue's blood."

"Any idea who it belongs to?" Boots asked, fearing the answer.

"More than an idea," Jimmy said. "The parents ID'd the jacket as belonging to Margo Steale."

"Well, it seems almost too convenient," Boots said, wondering if she was trying to convince herself of Steale's innocence. "But sometimes people kill without working out the details."

Boots looked around more, keeping her hands in her pockets like a good investigator until she was sure she had the crime scene imprinted in her memory. After giving the necessary assurances to Bryson that she would keep her unorthodox visit a secret between them, and that she would keep in touch, she left the scene.

As she was pulling away, she passed another unmarked car, undoubtedly on its way to the apartment of the late Lenny Blue.

Nineteen

Marc was grateful the alarm woke them up at seven. During their one hour of sleep, Penny had rolled back and forth as if she were at sea. Marc was the retaining wall, Penny's waves of distress beating him over and over.

They decided Penny should go to her apartment before Marc even left for his appointment with Daniel. This was a slight alteration of plans, but it seemed to make more sense for Penny to be in her apartment than for her to be holed up at Marc's until noon. Penny might even avoid some of the attention of the press by traveling during the anonymity of the morning rush hour.

"Marc, where's my jacket?" Penny yelled from the bedroom.

"The red one? I don't know," Marc yelled from the kitchen. "Is it under the bed?"

"No, I checked there." She pulled the bag into the living room. "Well, at least I don't have much to pack." She covered her face and started to cry.

"Sweetie, honey," Marc said, pulling her close. "I'm sorry this has been so awful."

"It feels like I turn a corner and find out that Lenny's dead. Then I turn another corner and find out again that Lenny's dead."

"Our minds can only process things in stages. It's just your brain trying to reconcile this." Marc stroked her hair; this was usually an erotic thing for him, but he was feeling far from amorous. "This is a dumb comparison, but after I got my wisdom teeth pulled, I kept feeling the holes in my gums with my tongue. It was like I didn't believe that my teeth weren't there anymore."

Penny stopped for a moment. "You're right, that is a dumb comparison. But it makes sense. It's okay," she said, pushing Marc away, "I've got to pull it together."

The cab arrived at seven thirty. "Well," Marc said, "I guess this is good-bye, for a while."

"Marc, you have been so great. I don't know what I would have done without you these last few days."

"Probably stayed engaged," Marc said.

She looked at Marc with warmth in her slightly bloodshot eyes. "I hope you never regret us." She looked down shyly. "I certainly haven't. I can't say that I wouldn't want to edit key portions out. This is going to sound like an Air Supply song or something, but I really didn't know that I could feel this way. I mean, I never really felt like this—"

Marc kissed her deeply. "Me either, Pen. Me either."

Twenty

Benjamin made himself a tiny pot of coffee in his Rogers Park home. He had enough grounds for one cup; he would need to go buy some more Chicago Nights blend from Moonstone Coffee and Tea later in the morning. The caffeine wouldn't help his nerves, which were already shot from the weekend's events, but he was hopelessly addicted to his morning buzz. He avoided watching TV, as it espoused too many conflicting, worldly values. He'd even refused to watch his appearance on last night's news. His only connection to the world, his subscription to *Chicago Lives*, was an occupational hazard. Since he worked in the entertainment business, he had to keep abreast of the movements of so-called culture.

He waddled out to his sidewalk to pick up the paper, and with cultivated discipline tucked it under his fleshy arm. He would read it with his coffee, not before.

He prepared his coffee with lots of cream, then sat down with the paper. He stared, mesmerized, at the cover story that hopscotched through the paper. His sister had created a publicity nightmare that he was unsure he would be able to fix, and with the death of Lenny Blue, he wasn't sure if it was worth fixing.

With the turning of the final page, he had knocked over his last cup of coffee.

* * * * * * * * * *

Boots would have loved to sneak back into Spooner's apartment and crawl into her bed, but she knew that she needed to get a jump on her day. Her stomach was upset. Probably because of so little sleep, she mused, reminded of the gentle, ample curves of Spooner's body. Boots knew that coffee would edge her already precariously upset stomach over the brink, but she also knew the little grocery store across the street from her apartment carried her favorite kind of bottled green tea. She entered the store, automatically looking at the headlines of the daily papers.

Chicago Lives stopped her dead in her tracks. She bought the paper and left the store, forgetting all about her tea.

* * * * * * * * * *

Daniel finished dressing. He left a message on his secretary's answering machine to cancel all his appointments except for his ten-thirty haircut, and made some notes in his laptop about his conversation with Marc and Penny. He loaded everything in his leather briefcase and walked down Lawrence Avenue toward the Metra train station.

He could have killed for some coffee, but he always held out for his espresso machine at work. However, this morning had already been out of the usual, so he found himself waiting in line at Doggy Doughnuts for a fountain Coke and an oat bran muffin to tide him over.

On his way out after his purchase, he passed a *Chicago Lives* newspaper machine. Frantically, he dug in his pocket for the right amount of change and grabbed the last copy from the display.

Instead of taking the train, Daniel hailed a cab.

* * * * * * * * * *

Gary left Daniel's apartment shortly after finding out about Lenny's death. Numb, he went directly home to his Lincoln Square apartment. He undressed, flopped on his bed, and stared at the ceiling for a long time. When he finally turned on the TV news in the bedroom, he watched two of the anchors of a popular local news show flip through the Chicago papers. And though they didn't discuss the lead article, the photo on one paper's cover was as plain as day.

Gary ran out to the convenience store on the corner, and spotted *Chicago Lives*. He proceeded to the counter, where he was told by the male proprietor that he would be arrested if he ever returned to the store in his condition.

Gary looked down and realized that he had run down the street and into the store, carrying his wallet but wearing only his boxer shorts.

He bought the paper anyway.

The same male proprietor, away from the aim of the video camera, discreetly slipped Gary his phone number.

* * * * * * * * * *

Penny unpacked her luggage, attempting to push aside her grief for Lenny, but for some crazy reason she kept thinking about her red jacket. There was no way to replace it. How many Denny's restaurants had that jacket been to? How she had loved that thing, even the small tear in the right pocket. Maybe it was a good thing that it was gone. Perhaps it would remind her too often of her times with Lenny and Gary, before everything got complicated.

Penny thought about the previous day's events. Her decision to face the press was, in hindsight, a poor one. Her intentions were to avoid looking like one of those people who covered their face every time a camera came up to them. It seemed more dignified. In the end, it made her look like a bitch. "Nice one, Pen," she muttered.

Penny knew she had to do something to keep herself busy before she went to Daniel's office at noon. For months she had planned to do this project. Now seemed like the right time. She pulled out cans of fabric paint and a large plastic tarp from her front hall closet. Pulling the large white sofa onto the tarp, she stripped the cushions and began to paint with large brushes and rollers, covering the blank surface with rich rust and tan, olive green and dark brown.

She was engrossed in her project when the doorbell rang. Cautiously, she looked out the spyglass. Nothing. She opened the door. A copy of *Chicago Lives* sat squarely at her door.

Funny, she thought as she picked it up, it should have been there earlier, when she got home. Maybe neighbors were helping themselves to her paper.

Then she saw the picture. "Goddamn them," she said, and shut the door.

* * * * * * * * * * *

Marc was tempted to take his Jeep downtown, but finally relented and reserved a car from Budget. He wouldn't be able to pick it up until the next day. Then he had called Boots and left the message that Penny had a lawyer, and who that lawyer was. D2 was a good friend of Boots's as well.

Those duties aside, Marc began the voyage thousands of Chicagoans navigate each day. After trying for fifteen minutes to flag down a cab, he decided to take a bus to the elevated train or, as millions of Chicagoans called it, the El.

Usually Marc found the castaway papers discarded by pilgrims who had traveled maybe only five minutes before him, crumbs of the *Chicago Tribune* or *Sun-Times* left behind by Good Samaritans who for some reason had read their fill or didn't want to be bothered by the paper anymore. But today, Marc couldn't even find the free papers or even *Chicago Lives*.

As he traveled, Marc told himself that he must be experiencing fatigue paranoia. Why else would he think people were staring at him? Never mind, he told herself as the train sped closer to the Loop.

* * * * * * * * * *

Spooner hated it when people left her bed before she left them. Boots had a good excuse, but still. She pulled a cigarette from the pack.

Last night, Boots had come into the bar. Spooner shouldn't have been surprised when, in the midst of coffee and discussion of Marc's plight, Boots stopped talking, leaned over, and kissed Spooner on the lips.

"I've been wanting to do that for a while now," was all Boots said.

Spooner was so taken aback that she forgot to kiss back. To amend, she grabbed Boots and they somehow ended up in bed together. She smiled, remembering how her skin had sung with Boot's caress, how Boots's coppery skin melted her inhibitions. "Damn," she said, and lit the cigarette. She wondered what Marc would think about this relationship.

"Marc!" Harsh reality burst through her memory as she wondered about Marc and this Penny mess. She put out the cigarette, rolled over, and got dressed. It was already late and she needed to get down to clean the bar. She hadn't wanted to keep Boots waiting last night. Then she'd go work out for a few hours.

She stumbled out her apartment door, picked up her neighbor's paper (who was on vacation), and walked a half block down Ravenswood to Balmoral. She dreaded the thought of dishes waiting for her, and as she unlocked the door she decided to break down and get a dishwasher.

As she opened the door to the bar, a kid came up behind her and hit her on the head with a board. Spooner's pilfered copy of *Chicago Lives* fell to the ground at the same time she did. Ignoring both, the kid pushed open the door and ran toward the counter.

Twenty-one

Marc arrived a few minutes late at Daniel's office.

"What a view!" he said. Marc said it every time he walked in. The office framed a good look at the Chicago River, and the Merchandise Mart glimmered as the large elegant behemoth it was. The sun shot back a brilliant reflection, and Marc shielded his eyes. "I'd toyed with the idea of moving down here, but there's too much light pollution. No chance of seeing the stars."

"I'm glad you made it," Daniel said with sincerity Marc didn't often hear.

"Hey, I've gotta confess, we changed your plan around a bit."

Daniel tried to cut him off. "Marc, I—"

"Wait until I tell you. Then you can yell at me." He took a breath and continued. "Penny's at her condo. She left before I did this morning. And she got there safe and sound. She rang the phone three times, then hung up. That was to let me know that everything was fine on her end. I hope that doesn't screw things up too much," he said.

"Marc, things are again a bit more complex. I am guessing you haven't seen *Chicago Lives* today." Daniel motioned for him to sit down next to his desk. The Monday issue was displayed so both could see it.

"Oh God," Marc said as he walked toward the desk, "now what? Picture of the mourning parents?"

"No, that's tame. They've gone after new flesh. Yours."

Marc was stunned. "They got a picture of Penny and me?"

"No, just you. And when I say flesh, I mean flesh." Daniel handed him the picture. "Go ahead, open your eyes. You might as well see it."

Oh, Sweet Mystery of Life/Death; At Last We Lost/Found You!

This weekend's breaking story has centered on the love gone bad story between Mr. Lenny Blue and Ms. Margo Steale, the two kids who were the toast of this year's Grammy awards. This storybook romance was aborted this week when Mr. Blue found his fiancée in the arms of another man.

This has been a disturbing story from the start, one that only *Chicago Lives* has dared to cover. A twisting story, filled with pathos, regret, and lust. And in light of the tragic death of Mr. Blue, the story adds "despair" to its list.

But first, about Ms. Steale's first lover, Lenny Blue. At press time, two unconfirmed theories into the death of Mr. Blue were circulating (Blue, page 3). Though the initial reports suggest suicide, police are conducting a full-scale investigation into a possible development suggesting homicide.

Meanwhile, an undisclosed source has just revealed the mysterious identity of Ms. Margo Steale's new lover. *Chicago Lives* was unable to confirm the name by press time, but we were able to confirm that the man pictured above is indeed Ms. Steale's new amour.

"My God," Marc said. He finally looked at the picture, a slightly hazy, out-of-focus head and shoulder—bare shoulder—shot of him.

Daniel knew the picture too well; he had stared at it during the long ride in the cab. "I hate to say this, Marc, but this is a damn good shot of you. Were it in another context, like in *Vanity Fair* or *Playgirl*, it would be quite flattering."

Marc was enraged. "It might as well be a centerfold. Where do they get this stuff?" Now that he saw it, he couldn't keep his eyes off it.

"That's what I'd like to know. Any idea?" Daniel asked.

Marc shook his head and then suddenly looked stricken. "Oh, God," he said weakly.

"Marc, don't tell me that you paid your way through college by being a porn star." Daniel was not in the mood for any new revelations about his friends.

"No, not quite. You see," he stalled.

Marc, you're killing me, Daniel silently pleaded. "Just tell me. Come on. It's not like I don't know you."

Marc put the paper aside. "I thought it was just a dream. On Saturday night—no, actually early Sunday morning—I answered Penny's doorbell. Whoever was there wouldn't stop ringing it. Anyway, this guy snaps my picture, assuming I'm Penny. Obviously he wasn't looking very carefully. When he realizes who I am, he says, 'Better yet,' or something like that, and takes off down the hall to the elevator. I shut the door and went back to sleep. I really thought it was a dream. Penny said I was sleepwalking, so I thought that it had something to do with that. But there's something else, Dan. A car followed us yesterday. After we left Penny's. Boots scared him off our tail. I wonder if this was the same guy."

"What is Penny's number?"

Marc told him from memory. Somewhat amazed that Marc had already memorized Penny's phone number, Daniel called her. He instructed her to pull all the drapes in her condo and not to open the door to anyone except for him. She said that she had seen the paper and couldn't imagine how they got a picture of Marc. Daniel quickly explained what Marc had just revealed, and that he would come over to her place around noon instead of vice versa.

"Penny saw the photo," Daniel said, putting down the phone. "She's upset about it." He tented his fingers in thought. "You didn't finish the article. It's probably better that you didn't. Anyway, they don't come out and name you, but they may have a good idea who you are. Or perhaps they're stuck and need a little help from their readership. It doesn't help that you have a glossy on the back of your book." Daniel waved his hands. "Not that any of this is your fault. If someone could just see me at three AM—" He stopped midthought but continued with his original point. "The fact is, all that strategizing we did earlier is probably for nothing. You might as well have come down in the Jeep."

"What a mess," Marc said. "It's almost uncanny how all of this stuff has surfaced."

"Only in *Chicago Lives*. And yes, on the local stations. The TV stuff is unavoidable in the case of the death of a public figure. But the coverage in that rag has been particularly sleazy. Penny was being tried in the press even before Lenny's death. I hope that this doesn't affect your teaching position," Daniel added.

"Good God, Dan, how could it not? Parents, administrators, they're going to know my face!"

"You could make a preemptive strike. Sue the paper. Accuse them of digitally manipulating their photos. Tell me, what did you wear to the door when you answered it? If you wore anything with sleeves, they're gone in this picture."

"I see," he said. "Like I said earlier, I ended up staying at Penny's Saturday night and, well, I wasn't prepared for a sleepover. I had my boxers on. I do remember Penny making fun of me wearing this frilly robe and, yeah, I must have grabbed it out of habit on the way to answer the door. It did have sleeves, but the neckline was a bit—" He stopped. "Ultimately what good would this serve?"

"They'll be forced to admit they altered the photo. I doubt that reputation is something they are too concerned about, but you can put a dent in their credibility. I can't promise that it'll help. It will force you to be open about yourself and will no doubt expose you as Penny's lover. And it could also muddy Penny's case as well."

"Talk about 'damned if you do, damned if you don't,'" Marc replied.

"Again, I'm probably not the best person to advise you on this kind of case. But I know a couple of good lawyers here at the firm who would be all too willing to take down *Chicago Lives*. Their stories have ruined plenty of people.

"But that decision can wait a little bit," Daniel said, getting out of his chair, leading him to the couch. "I do want to talk with you about Penny. I know that we both heard something last night we didn't want to."

Marc looked down. "Dan, about that stuff Penny said at the end. I don't think Penny killed Lenny. When she broke down, I think that the reality of his death was finally hitting."

"Before that happened, did you believe Penny was innocent?"

"Absolutely." Marc looked straight at him with clear eyes.

"But a few moments ago, you said, 'I don't think Penny killed Lenny.' You've downgraded your 'absolutely' to an 'I don't think.'"

"That was unintentional."

"I don't think so," Daniel said gently. "Marc, even the courts give room for reasonable doubt. It's okay to have suspicions. You should know that as a scientist. And suspicions don't always lead in the direction they seem to point. For Penny's sake, we'd better follow those suspicions and find out all we can before someone beats us to it. She was thinking about something—something she said or did to him and regretted. It may not have been a big thing, but it was something. We need to find out what that something is. No matter what it is. You follow?"

Marc nodded.

"I'm going to try to find out later what was going through her mind when she made that comment. But I might need your help as well."

"Then I can see her?" Marc asked.

"Yes, but be discreet, at least until we see where *Chicago Lives* takes us. If they zero in on your identity, discretion won't much matter. I can drop Penny off after I talk with her. Ultimately, the best way to get Penny off the hook is to find out what really happened to Lenny." Daniel scratched his head. "Penny, Lenny, Benny. It's weird how all these names morph into each other."

"Yeah," Marc said, "now I understand your frustration of having been with another Dan."

D1, Daniel mused, realizing he had not thought about D1 since the ball last Friday night. Three days. That was a record. "It takes some getting used to. Wait—is Penny Lane her legal name, or did she change it to match her stage name?"

"I couldn't tell you," Marc answered. "Sounds like a lawyer question to me."

"That it is," Daniel said, grabbing a pad of paper and pen from the coffee table. "I wonder about Lenny Blue as well. Sounds fake to me. Maybe *Chicago Lives* thinks that it can play with their lives because they are pseudonyms. Stupid logic, but it may be why they are running with it. It may also be the reason you were unnamed."

"D2, I'm glad you're taking this," Marc said. "For Penny's sake. It's such a bizarre thing, I'm not sure if I would trust anyone else."

Daniel put his notes down. "That brings us to the last issue. Marc, I don't know if I am the best person to do this."

"Dan, don't say that!"

"No," he said, "let me talk, and then you can yell at me. I, too, have a confession to make."

Twenty-two

The newsroom hummed, providing the background noise for a clandestine conversation by the coffeemaker.

"Any leads on Mr. X?"

"All nutty guesses. Of all the calls in, most name Denzel Washington or Will Smith."

"I'm surprised they didn't put Barack Obama in there as well. They don't look anything alike, or anything like the picture."

"Precisely. A few votes for Marcus Hawthorne. Then the others fall into the lesser known black male celebrity file. Then about forty people who claimed that they rode the El with him this morning."

"Wait. Did you say Marc Hawthorne? The science geek? Yeah, that's likely. Crazies."

"I know. We're pulling at straws here. So, what if we don't find him?"

"We will. Eventually. Or he'll find us. We're sure that photo is legit?"

"No doubt in my mind. Snappy's done good work for us in the past. He's a bastard, but he's good at what he does. In fact, he's actually got another story in the hopper. This one could blow way bigger than the Steale broad. It involves a certain alderman."

"Good, good. Now, what about those forty people who spotted Mr. X on the El? Where did they say they saw him?"

"On various lines, but most of them say on the Brown line. Could be something."

"The Ravenswood line, eh? He's out there. It's just too bad the chatty little Blue Man isn't around anymore to ID him."

Twenty-three

"The punk should have let me turn off the alarm first if he didn't want to get caught," Spooner said, resting uneasily in the hospital bed. "Stupid kid. At least I'm alive."

Spooner's head was swathed in cotton bandages. The board the kid had hit her with had given her a deep gash but had not fractured the skull. She had thirteen stitches. Though the doctor wasn't overly concerned, Spooner was to be kept under observation anyway.

"It's a good thing that you have a thick skull," Boots said, trying to hide her relief. Boots had been listening to her police scanner when the alarm was called in, and had seen the board. A rusty nail had missed Spooner's head by mere inches. "Don't get any bright ideas, missy. You're not leaving this place until they say you can."

"Who's gonna open the bar?"

Boots lowered her voice. "Screw the bar. You could have been killed, and you're worried that people will miss their evening beer? We'll deal with them later. How about you? How are you doing? I mean, really doing?"

"Well, I'm feeling pretty damn grateful to Marc for going behind my back and putting that alarm system in last month. But I'm certainly not going to tell him that. All I need is an 'I told you so' from the little shit."

"By the way, I tried to reach Hawthorne," Boots said. "He's not at home. I called D2 at his office. He's not there either. With the mess from the paper this morning, I doubt he's at Steale's—"

"What mess?" Spooner asked.

Whoops. "Now, I'm not supposed to upset you."

"That sounds like something straight out of *General Fucking Hospital*. What's going on?"

Boots smiled. Spooner certainly had a gift for language. She told Spooner about the story in *Chicago Lives* with Marc's picture. "It's a bit out of focus, and it's a weird angle, but people who know him will probably recognize him. Thankfully, they didn't name him. At least in today's issue."

"God, this whole mess is like sticky paper." Spooner tried to sit up. "Ouch."

"Quit moving around," Boots ordered. "Your brains might fall out. I was just getting used to having you around."

* * * * * * * * * * *

After she left the hospital, Boots jumped in her faux unmarked police car and for a second time that day shot down Lake Shore Drive.

In theory, the calendar had officially ruled in favor of spring. For once, the wind off Lake Michigan did not deny that assertion. Typically spring in Chicago was less a season than a two-week winter clearance sale in late April. This year the weather had been unseasonably warm for the Windy City. She passed Buckingham Fountain, the redesigned museum campus, the spiffy new Soldier Field, and plural McCormick Places as she headed to interview the parents of Lenny Blue. She reached the Fifty-third-Street exit in forty-four minutes, nineteen minutes longer than earlier in the day.

Hyde Park was an odd island of a neighborhood. Surrounded by communities struggling with poverty and crime, Hyde Park served as a startlingly clean and pristine backdrop to the prestigious University of Chicago. It was home to thousands of students, faculty, and administrators who could somehow afford its high cost of housing. Other independent schools and seminaries clustered around the austere gray monoliths to contribute to the neighborhood demographics of a highly educated population. Even though Boots had taken the U of C up on the scholarship they offered and attended there, she never quite understood the mystique. She had fled to the North Side of the city as soon as she graduated with her bachelor's degree and quickly switched gears from the theoretical world of prelaw to the realities of law enforcement.

Jimmy Bay had interviewed the parents Sunday night, but like so many others who lose loved ones, they were shocked into a state of unhelpfulness. This was likely unintentional. The bereaved often need time and space to understand their loss. Yet too much time is just as much a mistake, if not more. If too much time elapses, then sentiment or false guilt creates its own realities. Boots was never sure if she struck the right balance, but often the need for a timely investigation caused her to err on the side of opening fresh wounds rather than fading memories.

This time Boots found the house easily, sans police cars and yellow barrier tape. "Sandra Rudd." Boots held out her PI card when Mrs. Rantzhoff opened the door. "I appreciate your being willing to see me so soon after your son's death." Boots's words were to the point, yet her voice was compassionate.

"Come in." Minnie Rantzhoff led Boots into the living room and motioned for her to sit on a couch. "Would you like some coffee?"

"Thanks. I'd love some." Boots was amazed at her hostess's graciousness and felt guilty that she was about to excavate painful territory.

"My husband isn't home yet," Minnie added as she returned from the kitchen with a tray. "I had hoped that he'd be back from the paint store by now."

Paint store? The meaning suddenly became clear. "Mrs. Rantzhoff," Boots said, "I hope not to sound uncaring, but was your husband planning on painting Lenny's apartment? Because, see, even though the police have done an initial investigating, they may need to keep the apartment intact for a few more days."

"Oh dear, you're right," the woman said, unconvincingly. Her hands trembled as she seemed to understand the meaning behind the words. She asked Boots: "Cream or sugar?"

"Neither. Thanks," Boots replied, reaching to take the china teacup from an unsteady hand. "Mrs. Rantzhoff—"

"Please, call me Minnie," she said.

Boots hesitated, then complied. "Minnie, I know this is an awful request. But so rarely are we able to keep the crime scene intact—" *God*, Boots realized, *I still sound like a cop*. She started over. "If we keep your son's apartment the way it is for a few more days, it may help us understand what happened last night. We might learn something in a couple of days that changes the way we've looked at the room."

"I don't know," Minnie said. "Gerry can be pretty pigheaded when he decides something has to be done. But I'll tell him what you said. I mean, if he doesn't get here before you leave."

"That's all I ask," Boots said, catching Minnie's slip. Gerry Rantzhoff was not planning on coming home any time soon. The paint store had been a good excuse for him not to be home during Boots's visit. "If you don't mind, I'll take a look down there before I leave." Boots sat back in the couch. "Lenny was a talented musician. Did he grow up with music?"

"Both his father and I are musicians. Genetically he didn't have a chance." She smiled. "Gerry was a music professor at the university and he started Lenny off on music lessons, mainly piano. I was by no means a professional musician, but I helped out as I could. Lenny had the gift. During his rebellious times, you know, during his teens, he never touched the piano, but when he started Loyola, he picked it up again. Then he added guitar. That's where he formally learned songwriting, though he had been writing lyrics since he was a kid. Ten years later, after too many odd jobs to keep track of, he met Penny and Gary."

"Let's go back to his teen years. Was he a difficult teen?"

"No, not really," Minnie said wistfully. "Lenny has always had a moody side to him. During high school, he was a little more withdrawn. He read a lot, kept to himself. Actually, that's when we decided he needed some more space, and we finished the basement for him."

Boots was amazed that Lenny's parents had not been threatened by their aloof son and actually had given him greater independence. However, she did find it odd that a thirty-six-year-old man would have so few possessions in an apartment he had lived in for twenty or so years. "Did he keep his old bedroom too?"

Minnie appeared puzzled by her question, then seemed to understand. "Oh, you mean that Lenny's apartment seems a little barren. Lenny lived a very simple life. He didn't want a whole lot."

Boots considered herself a minimalist, yet even she had accumulated a significant amount of life clutter. None of that was present in Lenny's apartment. Minnie's explanation did not satisfy her. "What about his Grammy? Where did he keep that?"

Minnie pointed to a curio cabinet. "He gave us all the trinkets, knowing that we enjoyed being the proud parents—" Her voice caught, and then tears tumbled down. "I'm sorry," she whispered.

"Don't apologize," Boots said. They sat in silence for a few minutes. When Minnie was able to talk again, Boots asked her, "Did you have a good relationship with Lenny?"

Minnie nodded, wiping tears. "Lenny was a sweet boy. Sometimes a little cocky, but sensitive. When Gerry realized his son would never be the rough-and-tumble football-player type, he sulked for a few years, but eventually got over it." Minnie paused, opened her mouth as if to say something, but closed it. Boots wondered if Minnie's hesitation had anything to do with her husband's absence.

Just as Boots was formulating her next question about her suspicion, Minnie spoke again. "Lenny's always had good friends, and we were thrilled to death when he and Penny got engaged. We were, of course, as surprised by their engagement as everyone." Everyone being the millions of viewers who were watching the drama unfold on their TV screens.

Boots allowed Minnie to distract her from her suspicions, hoping to reintroduce her questions later in the conversation. "So you knew Ms. Steale?"

Minnie smiled. "Oh yes. We loved her and Gary like our own children. The three of them would come over for Sunday dinner together. When they weren't on the road, of course. Those times were the happiest of my life. I felt like I had adopted two more wonderful, fascinating children." Her eyes clouded in memory.

"Did something happen to change that?" Boots asked, sensing that Minnie had stumbled back on track.

"I'm not sure," she lied. "Gee, I wonder where Gerry is."

There was no sense in bullying the woman, so Boots didn't bother. She would tell if and when she was ready. "I'll not take much more of your time, Minnie. I do need to ask you if you think any one of Lenny's friends would seek to do him harm."

Minnie looked far away. "I can't imagine anyone who knew my son would do anything this terrible to him."

"Would he—harm himself?"

Minnie was silent for a long time. Then: "I can't say that Lenny hadn't dealt with personal demons. But I know he would not choose to die like this, in our house. Lenny would never have done anything like that. He knew. He knew that this would destroy us."

Boots looked at her. "Minnie, we still don't know what exactly happened down there. But you can't let this destroy you."

Minnie nodded. "I know." She was fighting tears. "You have no idea how this hurts."

"I'm sure I don't," Boots replied. A grandfather clock chimed the wrong time. "Minnie, I have one last question. Is there anything else that might help us find out what happened to Lenny?"

Minnie hesitated as she had done earlier. Then, to Boots's surprise, she slowly pulled a pair of keys out of her pocket. "Lenny came home Saturday morning. He did a couple loads of laundry. The keys must have fallen out of a pocket. I found them in the washer. I was going to give them to him Saturday night, but he didn't get home until late. Then on Sunday we didn't really see him until after—" Her silence finished her thought. They had not seen their son until after his death.

Boots took the set. The police had not recovered any keys, so this was a helpful break. Boots didn't think she needed to treat the set as if it was collected at the scene of the crime. And any fertile prints would have been compromised by the washing machine or by Minnie's handling of the set. Still, old habits were hard to break. Boots pulled out a plastic evidence bag she still happened to carry in her pocket and slipped them inside. Once they were safely inside the plastic pouch, she looked at them. A misshapen red leather cowboy boot gripped eight keys. She knew that she'd need to hand them over to Jimmy, though the thought of having them to herself was a surprisingly intoxicating fantasy. "Do you recognize any of these?"

Minnie nodded. "One is for his apartment downstairs. One is our house key. A copy of his car key. I assume one is Penny's apartment key. I don't know about the others. Maybe something to do with the band?"

"Are you saying this is a copy of Lenny's car key, and not the original?" Boots asked.

"Oh yeah," Minnie said. "I know because the original has the Honda emblem on it, and it's quite worn. This key is a copy, and a lot less worn." Lenny had owned a Honda Element, which, according to Jimmy's report, the Rantzhoffs hadn't seen since Saturday. The police had checked the neighborhood, and so far had not located the vehicle.

"So this is a duplicate set?" Boots was impressed with Minnie's detective skills.

"I think so. I don't ever remember seeing that key ring before."

They finished their coffee. Minnie led Boots down to Lenny's apartment. "I hope you don't mind if I don't go in," she said.

"Of course not," Boots replied. "I'll let myself out. Thanks for your help," she added, feeling the inadequacy of her words hang in the air as Minnie closed the door.

Boots always preferred viewing crime scenes in full daylight, as doing so somehow fooled her into accepting the organic nature of death. The sun rises and shines on both walls of paint and walls of blood. But this time no mental manipulation would help. She had just talked with the victim's mother.

Twenty-four

Just before Marc left, Daniel called Boots, but she didn't pick up. After leaving his office, Daniel took Marc into the record shop on the first floor of his building and found *Steale Away*, Penny's CD, located under the "Contemporary Christian" section.

Marc looked at the CD case and saw Penny's face looking back at her, with Lenny and whom he presumed to be Gary on either side of her. The name of the title track, "Steal Away," was immediately familiar to him, and the reason why Penny picked the song on the jukebox the other night was perfectly clear. "What an idiot I am," he muttered.

"What?" Daniel was distracted by the CDs in that category. "Hey, Marc, do you know any of these groups?" Without letting him answer, he continued. "I've heard a lot of these songs on the radio. I even have some of them on my iPod. Had I known ..." He trailed off in thought. "Insidious bastards. First they build ridiculous theme parks with the help of little old ladies' pension checks. Then they infiltrate the political system while hiding behind their tax-exempt status. And now this?"

"Amen, brother," Marc responded. "But I'm afraid you're preaching to the choir."

They made the purchase and left the store. Daniel sent Marc home in a cab. "And leave the Jeep alone," he reminded Marc.

Daniel kept his ten-thirty hair appointment at the Merchandise Mart, then returned to his office. Restless, he packed his briefcase and left. Within fifteen minutes, he rang Penny's doorbell.

"Hey," Penny greeted him as she opened the door.

"Did you check the peephole before you opened the door?" Daniel asked.

"Yes, I did."

"Good. A lot of vultures are circling downstairs."

She led him into the condominium. Daniel guessed that the place cost an amount in the high six figures, since his friends Jules and Pete had just bought a similar unit in the building and paid that amount. "Nice place."

"I guess so. My brother wanted me to have it," she said, anticipating his question. "It's part of the image he was building for me and Lenny. And of course he made the transaction without consulting me first. I treat it like a hotel room. Absolutely no attachment. That couch was the worst. This big iceberg in the middle of the Arctic."

The sofa was surrounded by open cans of paint on top of a large blue plastic tarp. Cushions were already covered with gentle swirls of pigment. Daniel thought it was a curious project to start at that particular time. "This is actually quite lovely," he said. "Are you an artist as well?"

"No, not really. I've been meaning to do this for a long time. And since I suddenly have a whole lot of time on my hands, I thought now was as good a time as ever. Frankly, I'm kinda surprised that it's turning out as well as it is. I was afraid I'd have to pitch it. Can you imagine dragging this thing out to the curb in this neighborhood?"

"If you don't like this apartment, why don't you sell it and get a place you like? Or get your own place and let your brother live here?" he asked.

"There's a really sick answer for that," she replied. "Lenny loves the place. You see, Ben consulted Lenny on what his ideal home would look like, and this is what the two of them came up with. He dreamed about the day he would move in here with me." She changed the subject. "Did I tell you that the place comes with its own personal Peeping Tom?"

"No," Daniel replied. "You did pull the drapes, right?"

"Yeah. Makes the place even more depressing. Benjamin's response? 'There's no way anyone can see this far.'"

"Bullshit," Daniel said. "Hasn't he heard of binoculars? Where does Tom live?"

Penny led him into the bedroom and pointed at the window. "Across the way. The window with dark drapes." She stopped.

"Penny, there are no dark drapes." All the curtains were either white or had white liners."

"I'm seeing that. Damn. I could probably guess, but now I couldn't be sure."

"That's probably what he was hoping," he said, and pulled the drapes shut again.

"Probably," she said. "Maybe he checked out and took his lovely drapes with him. That would make my day. Hey, have you had lunch? I hope not. I ordered some for us."

They ate in the kitchen. The restaurant delivered two pasta dishes and a large Caesar salad. Between mouthfuls Daniel said, "I guess I need to know a lot more about you, and about your relationship with Lenny."

"Sure. I'm sure one of the top questions is why I ever got involved with Lenny in the first place."

"Nail on the head," Daniel confessed.

"How long do you have?"

Daniel smiled. "I canceled my appointments for the rest of the day."

Penny took one more bite of food and then put down her fork. "After Iowa State, I decided that I had to give my music a shot, but I needed to move out of the middle of the cornfields. Frankly,

New York and L.A. scared me, I didn't think I was sophisticated enough to play the games. So I decided to move to Chicago.

"And I did okay at first. I played in coffeehouses, making just enough money to avoid getting the day job musicians always bitch about. I was doing this all on my own and knew that I needed some help if I really wanted to break out of the one-woman folksinger scene. So I advertised in the local alternative papers—you know, the *Reader* and *New City*—that I was forming a band.

"I met Gary first, and we hit it off from the start. He's a wonderful guitarist, self-taught, and could improvise your socks off. Not a songwriter, though he can turn a phrase or two, and not much of a singer. He's the first to admit that the best thing to do with him is to bury him in backup.

"Lenny was next. Like me, he has formal music training. He is truly gifted at marrying lyrics and music. He also has a terrific voice and harmonizes well. He plays guitar, piano, even Celtic pipes and some percussion if necessary. He was much more introverted than Gary and I, but he got bolder as he got more invested in the band. His style got brighter, lyrics less broody—though I don't mind broody—and by the end of the first year, we were playing well together."

Penny was talking as if Lenny were still alive. Daniel didn't correct her. "When did your brother jump in?"

"After the three of us had been playing for about two years. We hadn't broken past the smaller venues, though we were gaining a significant local following. Now, I know that you know little about me and Lenny, but you probably know even less about Gary."

Daniel had been taking a sip of water at precisely that moment. He swallowed it wrong and started to choke.

"God," Penny said, jumping up, "are you okay?"

"Yeah, yeah, fine," he said in a rough whisper. "Go on, go on, I'm fine."

She waited until his coughing subsided, then continued. "Well, Benjamin, my brother, had just finished his master's at a little school here in the suburbs, a dual degree in business and theology. Gary was the person that suggested Ben put the business degree in action and be our manager."

"That's an odd pairing of degrees, don't you think?" Daniel interjected. Then again, after what he had learned in the record store, nothing would surprise him.

"It is," she agreed. "It's actually ironic in a sort of Greek comedy kind of way. Or maybe it's more like a Greek tragedy," she said somberly. After a painful pause, she continued. "Either way, Benjamin and Gary have a hate-hate relationship that seems almost karmic. Gary thinks Ben had been controlling Lenny's life. On the other hand, Ben thinks Gary has been an evil influence on me. Up to a few days ago, he probably just thought that the language was the worst part. I can just imagine now.

"To be fair, Benjamin did work hard to get us gigs. We started opening for good bands—but eventually for more and more religious groups. Gary was never too happy about that. Luckily, we've always been able to maintain a solid following of Gen Xers, despite Benjamin's sway."

"That's what I don't get," Daniel said. "I've listened to your stuff, and it's not at all like the other religious stuff out there. What happened? Did Benjamin strong-arm the band?"

She stared over Daniel's shoulder for a good minute. "Have you ever driven along, thinking that you knew where you were going, but had gotten so distracted by your own thoughts that you realize you forgot to take the turn you needed to? The three of us were having such a good time with the music that we didn't really pay close attention to Benjamin. Suddenly the three of us woke up and found ourselves in a niche. If it weren't for the Grammy nomination, we never would have believed that we were being billed as a gospel group."

"You must have known about your brother's, well, tendency to be evangelistic about his faith."

"Oh, certainly. But we had made an uneasy truce—he left us alone, we left him alone. When we started to headline, he turned the tables on us."

"But you three were the musicians," Daniel said. "You should have had the ability to avoid his bullying."

"You would think that, wouldn't you?" she said. "But somewhere along the way, our coalition broke apart. It was weird. The three of us weren't as tight as we had been. Before, we'd had very fluid and open friendships, and although flirtation was a part of our stage act, it was just an act, or so I thought. After the Grammys and Lenny's proposal, it all fell apart. Suddenly our relationships were fixed. Lenny and I were engaged, and Gary saw himself as a fifth wheel. Instead of this sparkling humor that had always kept us moving forward during the hard times, he became sarcastic and sullen. I thought that maybe the pressure of the road was getting to him, or"—she laughed—"that he was maybe a little in love with me. How self-delusional."

"I'm guessing by that response that your friend Gary is gay, right?" Daniel asked casually. As if he didn't already intimately know that.

"He just came out to me on Sunday," she replied. "Before that, well, I guess I didn't pick up the cues."

"And how were you with that?" he asked.

"Well, I was fine with it. I mean, good grief, who am I to judge? I'm the star of the local scandal sheet!"

"That's not completely fair, but it brings up a good point," Daniel said. "This is completely off the subject and absolutely none of my business, but let me ask it anyway. On Friday, you are engaged to be married. On Friday night, you meet Marc and …" He hesitated. "And you seem to be fine with this. Would you say that this is an accurate picture?"

"I certainly can't say that I've thought through everything yet. I did date a guy for a while in the early days of the band, but my schedule didn't allow us to really have a fair go at it. I was focused on making a living in the music business. Then the proposal from

Lenny happened, and I decided that maybe I had put too much stock in the head-over-heels variety of love. I did have affection for Lenny, but it was much like my affection for Gary. And Lenny seemed to need me." She left the thought to dangle.

Daniel understood. A particularly common setup for women. "Well," he said, "it took me a year after my first relationship to acknowledge that I could be gay. Self-awareness certainly doesn't come overnight." *Sometimes it takes a few months*, he mused, and cleared his throat. "Have you talked with Gary or Benjamin, or even your parents, since Lenny's death?"

"No," she said slowly. "I don't think that I really believe it. It's almost like I have a concussion. And even though I didn't want to marry him, I still loved and cared about him as a friend."

"And," Daniel added, "you've really only known since, what, three this morning."

Penny's eyes veered slightly away. "I guess that hasn't been a whole lot of time, has it?"

Daniel touched her hand. "What were you just thinking about?"

"What?" she asked.

"I know that you were thinking about something. Listen, Penny—and I'm talking as a lawyer now as well as a friend—if this thing blows up, and I have to represent you, I need to know anything you have felt, heard, seen. It may not make sense now, but it could be the thing that exonerates you."

"What if I told you I killed him?" She looked right in his eyes.

"I'd have to say that I don't believe you," he replied slowly, looking right back.

"Well, good," she said. "I did not kill Lenny Blue."

"Was that a test?"

"Maybe. You never asked me directly. Probably because I'm involved with Marc. I thought that I'd get it out of the way for both of us."

"A hell of a way to do it," Daniel said, exhaling. "But you're not off the hook. I had just mentioned that you had only known since three AM. That triggered something."

Penny started playing with her food again. She had eaten very little. "I don't know if I can articulate it. I feel like I should have known something was up. And maybe I did. You know, I told you that I did go down to try to find Lenny but got turned around and lost. That part is true. I have been to his parents' home dozens of times, but last night I took the wrong exit and was completely turned around.

"I had also said that I didn't feel like I was in the right mind set to talk with him. I don't think that is accurate. It was more like a feeling of futility in trying to discuss anything, maybe because he was already dead. And I wonder if I had sensed that earlier, maybe he'd still be alive." She pushed her plate aside.

"Penny, are you sure that you're not trying to blame yourself for this? What you just described sounds a lot like survivor's guilt. It's when someone looks back, thinking that they missed an emotional signal, and slightly edits reality to point blame at themselves. Don't do that. It won't help you, and it certainly can't help him." He looked at her again. "There's more, isn't there?"

"Well, this is probably more of the same. On Saturday, when I broke up with Lenny, he alluded to something about why he needed to marry me, but I don't remember his exact words. It seemed important that we marry. I've tried to reconstruct our conversation, but Lenny's voice seems to fade. It's like even my memories of him are moving out of reach."

"It's very understandable. But that's the type of stuff you should probably talk with Gary about. I think Benjamin will have information, but it seems as if it may be slightly warped by his particular perspective."

Penny sat back. "I know that I haven't called them. But I wonder why I haven't heard from them either."

"Did you check your answering machine when you came home?"

"It was blank."

Daniel followed her to the machine. No calls.

Penny frowned as they returned to the kitchen. "Maybe they don't know."

"Oh, I would guess they know." *At least Gary,* Daniel added mentally. Why the hell hadn't he followed up with Penny?

"So, what are you thinking about?" she asked.

Daniel stood there, slammed into silence. In the space of a moment, he had let his professional guard down, something he would never do in a courtroom.

Just hours before, Daniel had told Marc about his own part in the drama, about the chance encounter with the man he named Cowboy. Daniel tried to convince Marc to find another lawyer for Penny. After much debate, they agreed it was better not to say anything to anyone, unless the worst-case scenario happened: that Penny was arrested for murder. In that case, he would find her a lawyer that could defend her in the courtroom with impunity.

Daniel mentally reentered the conversation with Penny. "I'm back in lawyer mode for a moment," he replied softly, staring at his hands. "You're going to have to trust me on this."

Long moments went by before he looked up at her. Her face could not disguise the blow he had just dealt her.

"Oh, Penny, this isn't about you. I just don't want to complicate things for you. Trust me. Okay?"

She relented. "I'm not sure what is going on. I just don't want to be the last one to know, okay?"

"Deal," Daniel promised, reaching out to touch her hand.

"God, I'm so self-obsessed. How's Marc doing?"

"Furious at that damn paper. He's sure that tomorrow's issue will give his identity away. And the only reason he's upset is that it compromises his position as a public school teacher. Now, you've probably figured out that Dr. A. Marcus Hawthorne could write his ticket at any university of his choosing. He turns away offers all the time because he loves teaching these kids. And now he's afraid that he'll lose his position at the school."

"This is such a screwed-up mess," Penny said. "And it's my fault."

"Oh, come on. No one—especially not Marc—is blaming you for that picture. If anyone is to blame, it's *Chicago Lives* for its lack of journalistic integrity. You don't see the *Chicago Tribune* or the *Sun-Times* pulling crap like this. Some of my friends leave the *V* out of it. They call it *Chicago Lies.* Sorry," he said, "you've just seen me on my occasional soapbox. And I almost forgot to deliver this from one Dr. Hawthorne." He pulled out a note and handed it to Penny.

"Here, I want you to have this," he said, pulling out a cell phone. "Carry it with you everywhere. I want to be able to get to you if I need to."

"I have a phone."

"I'd rather you not use your personal number. Besides, this one is in my network," he replied. "In terms of your rendezvous, I believe the instructions are there in the note. Before you go, I want you to try contacting your parents, Benjamin, and your friend Gary. You need all the support you can get." Daniel also wanted to hear what they would say.

He could tell Penny wasn't paying much attention.

"Did you read this note?" Her cheeks flushed slightly.

Daniel blushed back. "Just get the damn pink robe."

"Peach," she corrected.

Twenty-five

After Penny read the note, she ran into her bedroom and packed a bag. "A lot of hair care products, maybe?" Daniel asked. "Or are you preparing for a siege?"

"I know, it's a little big, but I couldn't find the smaller one. I'm usually not so bad about losing things, but this is the second thing I've misplaced in the last day—"

"What was the first?" Daniel asked.

"Oh, my red leather jacket. I'm not sure how I lost that. I practically live in it." She set the bag and her purse next to the door. "Okay, let's get the calls over with."

Daniel nodded. "I know that this isn't easy. But you need to stay connected for your own sake. And remember, this is not an easy time for them either."

"I thought of one other call I need to make. Lenny's parents," she said. "That'll be the hardest. They were always good to me. They probably hate me now."

"You don't know that."

She dialed Gary first. No answer.

Where is the little shit? Daniel wondered.

Then she dialed Benjamin's number. Gary was at Benjamin's, which explained why he pick up the phone when Penny called him. She spoke with Ben, then Gary, then hung up with a troubled look on her face. Apparently Benjamin found out about Lenny's death through the article in *Chicago Lives*, and said that he was still shaken by the news about her affair. Benjamin hadn't blamed her for Lenny's death, but he understood why Lenny would kill himself.

What a great brother, Daniel noted mentally.

Unlike Ben, Gary had asked how she was doing and said he understood that this was a bad time for her. Then he had said something that puzzled her. "It was unlike Gary," she said, reviewing the conversation aloud. "He said that because of the way things were, we should all keep a low profile. He was afraid of something, Dan, but I have no idea what that could be. Maybe he's afraid of being connected with me."

Daniel thought he understood. Gary was afraid that if he came into the picture, he would risk revealing too much and complicate Penny's already precarious situation. It was a sweet gesture, Daniel thought, but Penny needed Gary for support. If he was cautious, there was no reason why he couldn't be there for her. "Penny, would you call him back, explain that you have a friend who is a lawyer who would like to talk with him?"

She nodded. "But not with Ben?"

"I don't see your brother as being very helpful, at least right now. See if Gary can meet me tomorrow at my office."

She called back and relayed Daniel's message. Gary agreed to come to his office at one.

"Well," Daniel said to her, "two birds with one stone," referring to the call at Ben's.

"I wonder why Gary was there in the first place," she replied. "Two more to go." She called her parents in Iowa first. From the conversation, Daniel surmised they had not known about any of the events of the last two days, as their television was on the fritz. She told them first about Lenny's death, that it looked like a suicide but the police were investigating. Then she explained that Saturday she had called off the wedding. After some silence, she told them that she had discovered that she didn't love him the way he needed her to love him, and that she had found someone else. And in what Daniel dubbed a brave gesture, she told them that her new love interest was black.

"They were obviously stunned," she said after she hung up. "Iowa isn't the most integrated state in the Union. But I certainly didn't want them to hear it from *Entertainment Tonight* or what would have been even worse, Benjamin. Thank God I got to them first. Thank God that they have been too cheap to replace their broken TV or to install cable."

"Praise the Lord," Daniel said. "But your brother hadn't called them about this?"

She shrugged. "I guess that he's as messed up as I am. Anyway, I don't think this really hit home with them. They asked if I was keeping an eye on my little brother. As if this were just an ordinary check-in call."

After another deep breath, she dialed Lenny's parents. "Hi, Mr. Rantzhoff, this is Penny." Rantzhoff must have been Lenny's given name. "I can't tell you how sorry I am. Oh, okay," she said, waiting. To Daniel she said, "He's getting Mrs. Rantzhoff on the phone." Her attention went back to the phone; she repeated what she had said a moment earlier. She listened for a while, then said, "I don't know. I mean, I would love to, but I'm sure you've seen the papers … are you sure? … Yes, that's true, we did break up, but not in quite the same way as they said in the article … no, I think I've known for some time." She listened for a minute before speaking again. "If you're sure about this … okay, I'll be there tomorrow."

Daniel shook his head emphatically. She turned away. "Yes, I'll see you then. Bye."

"What did you just do?" Daniel asked, concerned that Penny keep a low profile and not do anything to further harm her credibility.

"They asked me to help them with the funeral on Wednesday. Even after they read about that garbage in the paper, they asked me to help." Tears dropped from her lashes.

"Penny, I'm sorry. I was being an ass. You certainly can help them plan a funeral. Hey," he said, putting his arm around her, "can you forgive me?"

She nodded and wiped away the tears. "It's just so sad. The whole thing is just so fucking pointless and tragic. You know?"

"I know." Daniel took her bag.

Twenty-six

Marc embraced Penny fiercely when she entered the hotel room, and Penny dissolved in tears again. "Sweetie, what's wrong?" Marc asked.

Penny couldn't speak, so Daniel did for her as he stepped into the room. "She just talked with Lenny's parents. Penny's going to help them with arrangements. Listen, I should leave you guys alone."

"Can you hold out for a moment, D2?" Marc asked.

Penny pushed herself out of Marc's arms and looked at him. "What's the matter? Are you okay?"

"I'm okay," Marc said. He wiped the errant tears off Penny's face. "After I left Daniel's office, I went home. Boots had left me a message. Spooner was admitted at Andersonville Hospital. She got caught in the middle of a burglary attempt. When she went to open the bar, she was hit in the back of the head with a two-by-four. Because the kid didn't know what he was doing, he tripped the alarm and was caught in the cash register. Spooner got a gash in the back of her head and plenty of stitches.

"As soon as I found out, I went over to visit. She's fine now," Marc reassured them. "Giving the hospital staff hell. You know, typical Spooner."

"I'm glad she's okay," Penny said.

"Why didn't I hear about this?" Daniel wondered aloud.

"Boots said that she called you too, but you were gone for the day. She asked me to have you call her."

Daniel pulled out his cell phone and called Boots. He spoke with her for about ten minutes. He put his phone away. "Good news. Spooner is doing fine. Bad news. Lenny's death had been moved officially from a suicide to a suspicious death. Autopsy results should be available later in the week. In the meantime, the police will start taking statements. They'll call to arrange a time for Penny."

Penny told Marc about her other phone calls, and about her plans for helping Lenny's parents with the arrangements the next morning.

"Don't worry," Daniel said, "the police can work around Lenny's funeral plans. I'll call them and change things if need be." Though he didn't want to say it, Daniel was grateful that Lenny's parents were allowing Penny into the process. That helped counteract the mountain of suspicion already building against her.

Marc added, "I'm sure they'll have plenty of people to talk with."

Penny sighed. "Not anyone with the apparent motive that I've racked up."

Daniel disagreed. "You'd be surprised at what resentments people hold against others. Those all factor in. Not that they in themselves prove anything," he said, waving his hands.

Marc sighed. "I'd imagine that Lenny and Gary's affair would factor into that."

"What?" both Penny and Daniel exclaimed, staring at Marc.

Marc looked stricken. "You didn't know? I thought that Gary told you the other night," he said to Penny.

Daniel mentally felt for the edge of the abyss, trying not to drop through. He wasn't sure if he was more upset as a lawyer or as Gary's love interest. "Marc, how the hell did you know about this? And why didn't you say something earlier?"

Marc turned toward Penny. "I thought he told you all of this when the two of you talked on Saturday. And Dan," he said, turning around, "I assumed that Penny would tell you about Gary, since he's in the band with her. I never gave this another thought until now."

"I can't believe he just blurted that out to you and hasn't told me," Penny whispered.

"It didn't quite happen like that, Pen. You had left the room, and Gary and I started to talk. He was apologizing for Lenny and mentioned how Lenny had once been a different person. He said it exactly as someone would defend an ex-lover. I caught his meaning. Then he asked me to let him tell you. Which I just blew. I'm sorry," Marc said.

Penny frowned. "He didn't, not during our talk, but I think he was trying to tell me. Also, Friday night, before the concert, Gary said he didn't think Lenny would be faithful to me. He wanted to talk to me after the concert, but I thought Gary was being melodramatic and didn't think much about it. I certainly didn't make it easy for him to say anything."

"Wow," Daniel said. "Guys, this is what I mean about how one seemingly little thing can completely blow up in our faces. At least for once, this is a complication that moves the bull's-eye away from Penny." But toward Gary, which complicated Daniel's situation completely.

Daniel got up. "I'll be sure to talk with Gary about this—"

Marc's eyes opened a little too widely.

"—tomorrow, when he comes for his appointment tomorrow afternoon at my office." He looked back at Marc calmly. "In the meantime, it's been a hell of a day. Get some sleep, okay? And lock the door behind me."

* * * * * * * * * *

It had been a hell of a day. However, instead of going home, Daniel headed back to Penny's building. He was able to confirm that Penny and Lenny had met at the downstairs restaurant Saturday afternoon, and that a few hours later Penny and Marc had dined at the penthouse bistro. Afterward, since he was already in the building, he stopped by his friend Jules's apartment.

"I'm sorry that it's so late, Jules."

"Hey, no problem," Jules said, closing the door behind them. "You appear to have been pretty tied up today. I missed our espresso break. No one makes it quite like you."

Daniel looked out the window. The view was almost the same as out Penny's window. "Does your building require white liners for your drapes?"

"Is this what couldn't wait until morning?" Jules asked. Not waiting for an answer, he replied, "Yes. It's part of the association's bylaws. But I don't know if that's true for the building across the way there."

"Why did you just mention that?" Daniel asked.

"It's a little thing called conversation. I recommend it highly."

Daniel pressed him. "There has to be a reason."

"Well, there is a guy across the way there who is a voyeur. Saw him jerking off one day in front of his nonwhite curtains. Daniel, why is this important?"

He shook his head. "It's not," he lied.

"So?" Jules prompted. "What's going on?"

Daniel rubbed his eyes. "I've got a problem, and I think I'm on shaky ground. I needed to talk it through with someone who would understand."

Jules motioned for Daniel to sit next to him on the couch. "You know, if this has to do with the brunette I saw you leave with the other night—"

"How did you know that?"

Jules smiled. "You can pull a fast one on Petey—and I know that, because I do over and over—but you can't with me."

Daniel ran his hand through his already tousled hair. "That man, the man I just had an incredible weekend fuck-fest with, is no other than the ex-lover of Lenny Blue."

Jules paled. "Lenny Blue, the musician?"

"Yep. And not only Lenny Blue, the musician. Lenny Blue, the man who died last night. And," Daniel said, getting up from the couch, "that's not all. It gets better. You know my friend Marc Hawthorne? Well, it ends up that while Gary and I were getting it on, so were Marc and Lenny's fiancée."

"Marc and Margo Steale? Your Marc is Mr. X?"

"And yours truly is representing Margo Steale."

Jules watched his friend pace. "So, you and this guy. Are you still—"

"No. I can't do it," Daniel said. "It's all too close. I can't see him while I'm representing Penny, er, Margo. It somehow feels wrong. Maybe after this is all done."

"And this Lenny. What was the deal with him?" Jules's voice was distant.

"You mean, about his death? The cops aren't sure what happened. They were saying suicide, but there's something that must not be fitting, because they are less conclusive."

"You don't think your friend—what's his name?"

"Gary. No, he couldn't have done anything. We were together most of the weekend. But I don't like being an alibi in this whole mess. I'm hoping it doesn't come to that."

"Then ride it out, Danny. See what the cards deal and go with it."

"That doesn't seem very proactive, Jules. I could be gambling with a lot here."

"For Christ's sake, Dan, you're not a fucking nun," Jules exclaimed. "Sometimes you just have to do what makes you fucking feel something, and take your chances."

Daniel looked at his friend. "Jules, are you okay?"

He sighed. "I'm fine. Sorry. I just get a little stir-crazy here sometimes without Pete. He's the one who keeps me on the straight and narrow. Well, maybe not so straight. You know what I mean."

Daniel knew precisely what he meant. Jules had a wandering eye. "I'm not sure that I want to pursue the obvious line of questioning. Pete's my friend too, and I'm not going to get in the middle of it this time."

"But Daniel, I think this time it would be beneficial to talk about it—"

"No, I don't. It doesn't matter. Whoever it was, it has nothing to do with me." Daniel headed for the door.

"In a way, you're right," Jules shot back. "At least this time, it doesn't have anything to do with you. God, are you still paying penance for our little indiscretion last year? D1 had just left you, and well, I had one too many at the office party. We both know it will never happen again."

"You're right. It won't." Daniel stopped and turned to his friend. "Sex really fucks things up, doesn't it?" He shut the door behind him.

Jules turned the dead bolt and nodded. Sex really did fuck things up. He returned to the couch and turned on the video to study the face of his last conquest.

Twenty-seven

Chicago Sun-Times
Leonard Rantzhoff, Musician

Leonard Rantzhoff, also known as Lenny Blue, songwriter and accomplished musician, died Sunday evening at the age of 36.

A Chicago native, Mr. Rantzhoff graduated from Kenwood Academy and received a bachelor's degree in music from Loyola University, Chicago. Mr. Rantzhoff continued private music study while teaching at the Old Town School of Folk Music. Mr. Rantzhoff is most recently known as the songwriter and musician who collaborated and performed with the group Save the Chukkas, a recent Grammy winner for Rock Gospel Album of the Year.

Survivors include his parents, Gerald and Minnie Rantzhoff.

A private funeral is planned in Chicago.

Chicago Tribune
Leonard "Lenny Blue" Rantzhoff, Award-Winning Musician

Leonard Rantzhoff, 36, recently known to millions of music lovers as Lenny Blue, died in Chicago Sunday evening.

Mr. Rantzhoff was born in Chicago. He composed his first lyrics at the age of ten, his love for music forming his subsequent educational pursuits. After attending Kenwood Academy in Hyde Park, he pursued studies in music at Loyola University, Chicago, where he graduated with honors. Most recently, Mr. Rantzhoff's songwriting and musical ability helped his band, Save the Chukkas, secure a Grammy for their album, *Steal Away*.

Mr. Rantzhoff is survived by his parents, Gerald and Minnie.

The family is requesting no flowers; donations can be made to the Lenny Blue Scholarship fund at Loyola University, Chicago, or the Blue Youth Scholarship.

Chicago Lives
Lenny Blue, 36

The life of Lenny Blue, musician and songwriter, ended tragically Sunday in the wake of allegations that his former colleague and fiancée, Margo Steale, had terminated their relationship and was instead pursuing an interracial relationship.

Mr. Blue's life will be celebrated at 12:00 noon Wednesday at the Family First Church, Chicago. This service is sponsored by Alive! Records and is open to the public. The first five hundred attendees will receive a collector's edition photo of Lenny Blue.

A private funeral is planned for family members in Chicago.

Twenty-eight

Boots recalled one of her mother's favorite sayings: Keep your friends close but your enemies closer. It was a peculiar thing for a mother to pass down to her children, but it was one piece of wisdom that stuck with Boots. One could never be too sure how folks come down in the end.

And for the line of work Boots was in, it was a particularly good piece of advice. She knew that the most cooperative, respectable people could commit the most heinous of crimes.

Until you can sort it out, it's just good to keep a good eye on all of them. Or have a trusted friend do it for you.

Daniel was exactly that kind of friend.

Boots called Daniel and found that Margo Steale was at the funeral home with the Rantzhoffs but would be returning to his office by noon.

At 11:18, Daniel greeted Boots in the reception area and ushered her into his office.

"Nice view." Boots barely looked out the window.

"Boots, why are you on this case?" asked Daniel. "I mean, has someone retained you?"

Boots shrugged. "Let's just say that it's personal interest. Anyway, we're on the same page when it comes to Hawthorne. I think we both want the best for him."

"I agree. Just so you know, we've all been following Marc's lead in calling Ms. Steale her given name, Penny Lane. It's less confusing. And more musical," he added, alluding to the Beatles song. "Seriously, because of our connections with Marc, I am aware that we need to keep this as aboveboard and professional as we can."

Boots looked at the coffee table, where she saw scattered pages from three of the Chicago daily papers. "I read them too," she noted. "Did something about them bother you?"

"You mean the obits?" Daniel asked. "Well, *Chicago Lives* has outdone itself in the tackiness department. Otherwise, I guess I was feeling relieved that Marc's identity wasn't given away. I didn't think about anything else. Though it does make me nervous. It would be just like *Chicago Lives* to blow this up on the day of the funeral."

Boots frowned. "I am assuming that you advised Ms. Steale—Ms. Lane, I mean—to cooperate with the police?"

He nodded. "She'll go in this afternoon to give a statement. Though we are hoping that Marc's identity as her lover will be shielded from the press."

"They will try their best, but the press have big ears. Regardless, neither Ms. Lane nor Hawthorne should need to identify themselves as lovers at this time."

"Penny will be referring to Marc as a friend."

"Fine," Boots said. *They'll need to be friends to get through this.*

Penny arrived about fifteen minutes later. "I'm sorry about the time," she said. Her face was a mask of pain. "That wasn't an easy thing to do."

Daniel made the introductions. "Penny, you're actually early, so there's nothing to apologize for. You've met Boots, er, Sandra Rudd, right?"

Penny looked like hell. "I'm sorry that we had to do this now," Boots said as they shook hands.

"Hey," Penny said, trying to be gracious, "it's okay. No time is turning out to be a good time for this. Both Marc and Dan have said a lot of good things about you."

They sat down. "Well," Daniel said, "let's get this over with."

Boots nodded and began asking Penny general information leading up to the events of Sunday evening. "Now, in terms of Sunday, would you tell me exactly what you did between five PM and midnight?"

Penny recalled she had gone home with Marc, where they had watched the early evening news. She had seen her brother give an impassioned plea for her, and went to speak with him about it. Not finding him there, she visited his church, where he was at the podium. After his pointed words toward her, she left. She had planned to visit Lenny, but after getting turned around in Hyde Park she just drove around the city for about two hours, then returned to Marc's apartment. Marc was asleep and did not know she was home until two thirty.

"What time did you visit Family First?" Boots asked.

"Oh, a little before eight." She looked uncertain.

"Hmmm," Boots said. "So the gap would be between six and eight, and then from eight until your friend Mr. Hawthorne woke up and saw that you had returned."

"That's right."

"Where's the Jeep now?"

Daniel answered, "Marc was advised not to use it."

"Fine." Boots followed his thought. Since the Jeep was Hawthorne's, it could be identified. "I can tell you now that the police will ask to look at it. Hawthorne should not drive the car until they clear it." She stood up.

"Is this it?" Penny asked.

"For now," Boots said. "Just to warn you, the police will be more exacting. When I have other questions or need to get a hold of you, I'll call. Dan gave me your cell phone number," she added as she shook their hands and left the office.

By the time Boots retrieved her car, it was 12:45. She calculated that she had just enough time to grab lunch before her next appointment. She raced up Lake Shore Drive toward Rogers Park.

Twenty-nine

After Boots left, Penny broke into tears.

"Hey," Daniel said, "you did fine."

She shook her head. "No, it's not that. It's just that everyone has been so nice. Lenny's parents. Marc. You. Even Boots, for God's sake."

Daniel offered her some tissues, and Penny blew her nose. They sat in silence for a few moments until her tears stopped.

"Penny, I'm expecting your friend Gary in a few minutes. You don't have to leave just yet, but I need to ask you a big favor. Another one of those 'trust your lawyer' favors. Don't tell him that you know about his affair with Lenny. Okay?"

"Dan, if you're planning on pinning murder on Gary just to save my hide—"

"No, no," Daniel corrected. "That's not what I'm planning to do. I just don't want him to be on the defensive. I need for him to tell me about this. Again, trust me. I am not going to set him up. Okay?"

She looked at him. "Okay. I can leave now, if you want."

"I would like you to stay for a while. Introduce us, and that kind of stuff. Break the ice, you know. Then the three of us can go to the police station together. If you don't mind, you can wait in the reception area or one of the other offices while I talk with Gary. Speaking of which, I'd better check the waiting room. What does he look like? I can't seem to remember from the Grammys," he lied.

"Gorgeous," she replied. "I doubt anyone else in your waiting room fits that description."

Don't I know it? Daniel added mentally.

"Mr. Weaver, Mr. Cowboy is here to see you," the receptionist said nonchalantly as Daniel walked out the door.

Daniel must have inadvertently given the receptionist Gary's nickname name when setting up the appointment. "Betty," he said, trying to gain his composure, "I'm going to send Ms. Lane out in a moment. Would you set her up in Mr. Merchant's office until Mr., uh, Cowboy and I are finished? Mr. Cowboy, would you like to come in?"

Gary got up from his seat. "Good to meet you, Mr. Weaver," he said, smiling sweetly as they shook hands.

Daniel said softly, reining in control again, "Penny is in there. She doesn't know anything. Let's keep it that way, okay?"

Penny and Gary rushed into each other's arms like lovers. Daniel fought back an irrational fear of jealousy. "So," he joked, "you two know each other?"

Penny broke away. "Oh, I'm sorry, Dan. Daniel Weaver, this is Gary Davis. Gary, Dan."

"Well," Gary said, "it's good to meet you." He turned to Penny. "Is he treating you okay?"

"He's great," Penny said. "He's a friend of Marc's. They've both been wonderful."

"I'm glad. This whole thing is a mess. And what happened to Lenny, well …" He trailed off.

Daniel gave Penny a visual nudge with his head. "Hey," she said, "I'd better go. I'll see you in a few," she added, looking at Daniel.

He nodded. "Get outta here," he said playfully.

She hugged Gary again, then walked out the door.

Daniel counted to ten to make sure that she had really left, then said to him, "You knew about Lenny's death since early Monday morning. Why didn't you call Penny? Why did she have to call you?"

"I couldn't," Gary said, flopping on the couch.

Daniel didn't sit. "She has been attacked by the press relentlessly. Her brother has practically sentenced hellfire on her. Then her ex-fiancé is found dead. She needs someone who is supportive. She needs you."

"But I thought that I would complicate this—"

"I knew it!" Daniel said. "Are you avoiding her because of us? Because you might slip and she'll find out? Because that's sweet, but completely misdirected." Daniel sat next to him. "I know that she needs you to be there for her. And I think you need her too. Just be cautious. Okay?"

Gary sighed. "Blondie, it's been hard. It's killing me not to be with her. She's like a sister to me. She has been the absolute best friend I have ever had. You know I only came out to her Sunday? I was so afraid that she would hate me."

"Why? Because you're gay?" Daniel asked.

"Well," Gary said, moving slightly away, "it's a little more complicated than that. And she doesn't even know all of it. You see, before the Grammys, Lenny and I were lovers."

Well, good for you, you said it, Daniel said silently. "Penny doesn't know about this?"

"No. I tried to talk her out of the marriage thing, telling her that they were all wrong for each other, but she held firm. Finally, Friday, I decided that I needed to tell her and was going to meet her at her place after the concert. Except she left early and never came back. I called to check in with her, even stopped over at her place, but she wasn't at home. I ended up at the benefit instead. It was me, chickening out."

"She never went home last Friday night," Daniel reminded him.

"Yeah," he said, not wanting to let himself off the hook just yet. "And then Sunday, when I came out to her, I had another chance. But I just couldn't say it."

"Did you still love Lenny? I'm mean, until—"

Gary shook his head. "It could never be the same again. When he proposed to Penny, I felt like I had been slapped across the face. Penny knew something was up, but I couldn't tell her that her fiancé had been fucking her best friend."

"According to Penny, both you and Lenny changed after the Grammys," Daniel prompted.

"By the end there, I wasn't liking myself too well, mainly because I was letting Lenny screw over Penny. I was so angry at him sometimes I wanted to kill him." He stopped; tears gathered in the corners of his eyes. "I can't believe he's gone, Dan. Not like this."

"Gary, it's okay," Daniel said uselessly, kissing him softly on the top of his head. "Go ahead," he said, feeling frustrated that he couldn't relieve Gary's pain.

Or his own. Crying cowboys made Daniel horny.

Thirty

Boots thought it unfortunate that Penny's alibi was less ironclad than her brother's. She also thought it unfortunate that the only person that could substantiate Penny's claim to be on the North Side of the city claimed he didn't see his sister the night of Lenny's death.

"Come in, come in," Benjamin Lane had said after Boots flipped open her wallet and identified herself. She was a bit early.

He directed her to his living room. "Do you care for anything?" he asked. "I just made a fresh pot of coffee. Chicago Nights blend—from Moonstone's," he added, somehow thinking that the brand name made it more appealing. "Freshly ground yesterday."

"I'm fine," she said. "Go ahead and fix yourself some."

He disappeared, and Boots looked around the room. She hadn't seen such an antiseptic room since her early Sunday school days. Each wall contained at least three framed Bible verses. Some of them seemed more damning than inspirational. She was not surprised when she spotted the ubiquitous "Footprints" poem hanging among the others.

Boots sensed him return to the room. "You are quite devoted to your faith, aren't you, Mr. Lane?"

He motioned her to join him on the couch. "Officer, it's always good to remember where 'home' is." He set off "home" with finger quotations.

"Actually, I'm not an officer," she replied. When she had set up the interview, she was very clear about that.

He waved her again toward the seat next to him on the couch. "Right."

She veered from the couch to a wingback chair. "That brings me to my first question, if you don't mind us just jumping in. I saw you on television on Sunday, asking your sister to come home to the Lord."

"That's right, ma'am."

"At about what time was that?" Boots could tell that he thought her question was going to take a different direction, and she caught him off guard.

"Uh, what time?" he asked.

"Yes." Boots did not smile.

"Well, let's see. I read the paper in the early afternoon—I slept in on Sunday, but don't 'tell' on me—and the story about sis 'hit' me right in the face so hard I couldn't believe it. I called Lenny, and he came 'over'—that must have been around two or so." Again with the finger quotations, Boots noted.

"You called Lenny, but not your sister? Why was that, Mr. Lane?"

"Are you familiar with the Holy Word?" he asked.

Boots stopped looking at his hands altogether. "I'm familiar with the book. I had some teachings on the reservation," she added, trying not to grimace.

"Ah yes," he said with a knowing look, "of course."

Boots knew that she had just been classified as one of the heathen who had been brought into the fold. Though she didn't relish the idea, she didn't correct his perception. "So, about your sister?" she prodded.

"Yes. Luke 8. Jesus' mother and brothers come to Him, trying to get through the crowd. What does He say to the disciples when they tell Him of His family's 'dilemma'?"

Boots sighed and picked up the gauntlet: "'And He answered and said unto them, My mother and my brethren are these which hear the word of God, and do it.' Verse 21," she recited. Boots had memorized the whole book of Luke to earn a free scholarship to Bible camp. Though Bible camp was less than a pleasant experience, at least her memorization was finally paying off.

"Well, well," he replied. "A perfect recitation of the Authorized Version of the King James Bible. Quite admirable." Benjamin continued. "The point is, of course, that blood is not always thicker than water—if that water is of the 'true baptism.'"

True brainwash, maybe, Boots assented. "So, you invited Lenny over. And the two of you talked?"

"Yes. He confirmed the truth of the story. That sis was, well, 'you know,' and that the engagement was 'over.' Mainly I just listened to him."

"Of course." She wanted to ask him how long he had been a fucking bigot, but she figured she wouldn't get very far taking that approach, so she kept her cool. "And Lenny was here for how long?"

He sat back, rubbing his chin. "Well, I'd say until about three thirty or so. After he left, I was so upset I needed to talk with sis, 'straighten' this mess out. So I went down to her place but never got past the doors. The management thought that I was from the media and wouldn't let me in."

"Thy brethren stand without, desiring to see thee," Boots quoted sweetly. "Luke 8:20."

"Uh, yes." He was visibly impressed.

"And how long did you wait for her?" Boots continued.

"Maybe about an hour. That's about right. She left sometime before five. And I didn't even get a chance to really 'talk' with her."

She got the message, Boots added silently. "And then, after you gave the statement to the media, what did you do?"

"Well, since I was already parked there, I decided to eat at one of the restaurants downtown. I was there until about quarter to six. Then I drove to church, since I was to preach that evening. Did you know that I was 'ordained' at that church?"

"No. That's fascinating," Boots replied with little fascination in her voice. "And you went to the church?" She nudged him back to the subject.

"I got there just as the groundskeeper was opening the door. That was probably around six thirty. The service started at seven, and I was there until about nine. I 'preached' between about seven fifteen and eight."

"And you were there the whole time—between six thirty and nine?"

"Yes," he said too quickly. A slight hesitation, then, "Well, not quite. You see, I was running out of coffee, and there was a Moonstone's right across the street. I ran out for just a few minutes to get a fresh pound. I was gone for maybe fifteen minutes."

"Before or after your sermon?" she asked.

"What? Oh, before," he said.

Boots didn't need a polygraph to know he was lying. "I won't bother you too much longer," she said. "You've been very helpful. One last thing. When is the last time you saw your sister?"

"I haven't seen her since Sunday outside her building."

Boots got up to leave. "Thanks again for your time. If you think of anything you forgot to tell me, please call me." She gave him her business card.

"I preach every last Sunday of the month at Family First," he added. "Why don't you come by sometime?"

Was he hitting on her? "Thanks. Maybe I'll see you at the memorial service tomorrow."

"I'd like that," he said with a wink, and shut the door.

Yuck, Boots thought as she climbed into her car.

* * * * * * * * * * *

Jimmy Bay was already waiting for her at their usual coffee shop, which was on the one side—the Chicago side—of Howard Avenue, not far from Benjamin Lane's home. On the other side of the street was the city of Evanston, which boasted Northwestern University, football miracles and debacles, better school funding, and higher tax and income brackets than its more southern neighbor.

"Just talked with Benjamin Lane," Boots said as she slid into a familiar booth with the all-too-familiar Formica top. "That guy gives me the creeps."

Jimmy smiled. "Most guys give you the creeps."

Boots ignored his baiting. "What's happening with the autopsy?"

"As usual, the morgue is booked. But because Blue's a high-profile case, Bridge'll get him in under the knife this afternoon—actually, in just over an hour. Bryson and I'll be there. They're rushing the blood work too. Figured that we'll hear more tomorrow."

"And the keys?" Boots asked.

"Interesting, but not too helpful. Here's a copy of the set," he said, sliding a ring of eight keys across the booth to her. "The four marked are the ones Mrs. Rantzhoff named. Lenny's apartment, their home key, his car—or at least what looks like his car key, since we still haven't found that. The fourth one fits Margo Steale's condo. Those other four keys could be for anywhere. Nothing distinctive about them at all. And of course, any prints were worthless. And of course, I never gave them to you. Understood?"

Boots nodded and ordered coffee. "Did they find anything on the jacket?"

"A lot of stuff, but most explained by a bloody coat being stuffed in a Dumpster with a bunch of dirty diapers and old food. A few fibers from other Dumpster junk, but no leads."

"None of the neighbors reported anything suspicious?"

"Just the one who heard the gunshots." Jimmy said as they both watched a familiar car squeal around the corner. "Uh-oh. Here we go again."

"What I don't understand is that a guy gets shot and no one in the neighborhood sees anything suspicious. No one is walking their dog, or going home from the movies, or whatever." Then standing up, she asked, "Radio for backup?"

He nodded as he reached his for holster. "Hyde Park is still on the South Side, Boots. Folks don't go out much after dark. Ready?" He followed her from the table as he spoke into his radio.

Just as they positioned themselves behind the door of the restaurant, a large white man with startlingly white hair and a grizzled beard barreled through the door with a shotgun. "Where are they?" he yelled, pointing the gun over the heads of the few customers in the coffee shop. "I know they're in here."

Before he could turn around, Jimmy's gun lightly touched the man's head. "Put down your piece, Klinger," he said quietly. "And don't try any moves. Hot Lips is right here, backing me up."

Boots added her gun. Actually, her finger. She had lost her right to carry last year.

The man put his gun on the floor and slowly stood back up. "All I wanted was the Section Eight, Colonel Potter," Klinger said, blinking, his delusions settling down as the reality of arrest settled in.

Jimmy (a.k.a. Colonel Sherman Potter) and Boots (a.k.a. Major Margaret "Hot Lips" Houlahan) had been players in Robert Clayvey's (a.k.a. Corporal Max Klinger's) fantasy world since their rookie days. In his medicated state, Clayvey was a custodian for a local engine factory. Unmedicated, Klinger was trapped in a mountainous *M*A*S*H** unit in Korea. It was a plight Clayvey/Klinger knew intimately, as he watched the reruns of his life every night on TV. He had never personally seen Korea or Vietnam.

"Maybe your name should be Radar," Boots/Hot Lips said to Clayvey/Klinger. "How do you always know we're here?" she asked the too frequent offender. He didn't answer her.

"We should show him the final episode," Jimmy muttered under his breath, thinking that closure might move him out of his fantasy. They both feared the day when his mental illness would extract lives. His gun never had been loaded in the past, but who knew when that piece of the scenario would change? They walked the confused soldier to the squad car they had just radioed. "The usual," Jimmy said to their old colleague, Wynston Smiley.

As usual, Smiley grunted and took Clayvey out of their custody. "Just what I needed today," he growled as he put Clayvey in the backseat.

"Jimmy, don't you just miss the old neighborhood?" Boots asked.

"Yeah," he replied, "I'm feeling pretty damn nostalgic right about now," he added as he jumped into his squad car and headed toward Cook County Morgue for his front-row seat at a late afternoon autopsy.

Boots sighed and followed the other squad car. Since Jimmy had another engagement, she knew the rest of her afternoon would be devoted to recording their part in Clayvey's latest episode. This was another in a long series of times she wished she could trade places with her ex-partner.

Thirty-one

Daniel accompanied Penny and Gary to the Twenty-first District of the Chicago Police Department where the two living band members gave their sworn statements. Since there was no compelling evidence that either one had committed a crime, they were allowed to leave, with the understanding that they would not be taking any road trips any time soon. They left the station, and Daniel dropped them both off at Penny's condo.

Next, he went to the Old Starlight Hotel, where Marc and Penny had stayed the night before. Marc had a three-thirty meeting with his school's principal, and Daniel offered to accompany him.

"This is probably not a good time to ask you this, Marc," said Daniel as they drove back down to the South Side where his school, Hancock Academy, was located. He shook his head. "Never mind."

"What?" Marc asked, hoping for a distraction.

"Well," Daniel said, "when I went over to Penny's yesterday, she was in the middle of a project. She's painting her couch."

"Not with house paint, I hope," Marc replied.

"No, she's using fabric paint. And frankly, the result is quite stunning. But it just seems like an odd project to embark upon in the middle of all this."

"Daniel, she hated the couch. She hates the whole damn place. She's probably trying to occupy her time."

"You're right. Just a silly question."

The couch mystery would not have bothered Daniel had he not read *Chicago Lives* earlier that morning. They had dug up one juicy morsel not run by any of the other papers. Allegedly, Lenny did not die in his basement apartment. His body had been moved there after death. Of course, Daniel assumed he should take anything he read from *Chicago Lives* with a gigantic grain of salt. However, if the paper was right, Lenny Blue had died somewhere else. Had he died on Penny's couch? Was her "project" a way to cover evidence of Lenny's demise?

Daniel's mind silently tallied up more suspicions. Penny had moved the couch over the tarp. The couch was pretty heavy. Was Penny strong enough to move a dead body? His instincts told him Penny had not killed Lenny. But suspicions are hard to dismiss.

There was another problem Daniel faced. He had made two serious slips around his relationship with Gary Davis. The first was on Monday when Penny had caught him off guard. He had been wondering why Gary hadn't called her, and she sensed that he was withholding something. The second was earlier that morning, when he had mistakenly given his receptionist Gary's nickname instead of his real name.

Daniel was getting sloppy.

When he discussed the dilemma with Marc, they decided that the situation didn't necessarily compromise his ability to handle Penny as a client. Daniel had been uneasy about this, but assented. Hadn't he just given a similar line to Gary a few hours ago? "Just be cautious," Daniel had said to Gary.

Too bad he wasn't taking his own advice.

Daniel had never placed himself in this situation before. Sure, he had friends who were clients. But he never was in the precarious position of being intimate with a friend of a client. And not only a friend of a client, but a possible suspect in a homicide case. And not only a suspect, but a suspect who had been intimate with the dead ex-fiancé of the client.

But Daniel put both of these things out of his mind. He turned his attention to Marc beside him. He was barely containing her nervousness. "Hey, Marc," Daniel said, "don't worry. You'll be fine." He knew he was lying, and so did Marc. "Whatever happens, we'll make it through," he added. At least he wasn't lying about that.

* * * * * * * * * * *

Principal Shannon Doyle sat behind her desk and directed them to the chairs facing her. The diminutive seats were strategically placed to intimidate ill-behaved kids. The seats were no less intimidating to Daniel and Marc. They had the additional disadvantage of their adult size. Marc, in the high-five-foot range, negotiated the chairs slightly better than Daniel at six-foot-plus.

"Thanks for coming down on such short notice," the principal said. Doyle was closer to Daniel's height than Marc's and a solid, no-nonsense demeanor defined her plain face and sensible, attractive, and expensive gray tweed suit.

Marc recalled the old saying that taught millions of children the way to keep the spelling of principle and principal straight: the princi*pal* is your pal. Marc had enjoyed a good working relationship with Shannon Doyle. He only hoped that Shannon would continue being her pal. "Is there a problem?" Marc asked.

"Marc, let's not be coy. I think you know what's up. Why would you bring your lawyer if you didn't anticipate a problem?" The principal sighed. "I have gotten questions from about a dozen parents about that picture in *Chicago Lives*. And frankly, I'm not sure how to handle it. I don't want to be adversarial about this."

"May I?" Daniel asked Marc. Marc swept his hand in permission. "Principal Doyle—"

"Call me Shannon."

"Okay, Shannon," Daniel replied, looking to Marc for guidance. Marc nodded, giving him permission to speak frankly. He did. "This conversation is strictly off the record. Frankly, we don't know quite how to handle it. We're not going to pretend that it isn't a picture of Marc, though we're not sure how they would even have gotten a shot like that. Obviously the picture has been altered, so that we could have a strong suit against them. But this would entail revealing Marc as the subject of that photo. Since they did not run a follow-up story, we are assuming that they are still unsure who is in that picture."

Shannon assessed the situation quickly. "So it's trying to anticipate whether or not *Chicago Lives* will uncrack the mystery."

Marc added, "Shannon, it's likely they will. The question is whether to take the offensive or the defensive." He looked away. "Either way, parents will figure this out. The ones who don't already know will know soon enough."

"If this were only an issue of sexual partners, it'd be tough but we'd be able to deal with it. But that damn article places you in some very murky water, none of which is any of my business, and I don't want to know anything about it. If nothing else, the photo frames you like some kind of porno star." Shannon sighed, and they sat in silence for a long moment.

"You are the best teacher I have ever had," Shannon continued. "Maybe that's because you choose to do this, where so many others feel like they are forced into it. Students love you. Parents are excited when they see you challenge their children to achieve. And God, without the grant monies, how else would a public school ever afford to pay for a scientist who has worked for NASA? Most of all, you truly give a damn about these kids. But with all that aside," she added, looking at her desk, "I have been requested by the local school board to strongly advise you to take a voluntary leave of absence until this all is cleared up."

"Shannon, you realize that the LSB's demand for a voluntary leave is contradictory." Marc's commentary belied his frustration. "What if I don't?"

Shannon Doyle continued to stare at her desk. "Then I've been instructed to ask for your resignation. I'm sorry, Marc. I have no choice in this." Her eyes finally met Marc's.

"I don't think the LSB can do this, can they?" Marc asked Daniel.

Daniel shrugged; he had little at-hand knowledge as to the limits of the local school board. Marc continued. "Do they realize that the AASF grant that funds the science project is tied to my presence at the school? That the funding and the assets would leave with me?" The African-American Scientist Fund had granted Hancock Academy a three-year grant to raise student awareness of the sciences through the placement of a prominent black scientist as their teacher. Hancock Academy had won that honor and was not even one full year into the study. "Shannon, that includes all the equipment, including the school's planetarium."

"If they pull this project," Daniel added, "Hancock will have slim to no chance at any private monies again. It will ruin the school's reputation within the private and public sector for years. It will also set back a project like this for any other schools."

Marc could tell by the defeated look on Shannon's face that she was all too aware of these realities.

"The board believes that their decision is the best way to protect the reputation of the school."

Shannon continued. "I hope you know that I fought against this decision. It was a compromise to suggest that you take a leave of absence. They asked me to fire you. I told them they'd have to fire me first, because I wouldn't do it." She pulled a hangnail from a hand that was already suffering from similar assaults. "Please, Marc. I'm asking you as a friend and colleague. Take the damn leave of absence. Give me some time to rally some support with the parents. Maybe we can resolve this, somehow salvage all the work you've done this year."

Daniel stood slowly. "I'm going to ask Marc to delay his decision on the voluntary leave until we discuss this with some of my colleagues. And again, this is off the record, Shannon, but I don't particularly like the options Marc's been given. I'm not sure if he would be better served by the courts if he took a leave or if he was outright fired by the LSB. Both victimize the victim, either by having him remove himself from the classroom for alleged misconduct or by submitting to an unjust termination by a board of myopic people."

"Marc," Shannon said. "I'm sorry."

"I know," Marc replied. "I know," he said as he stood to leave.

* * * * * * * * * * *

Marc stood outside his classroom door. "You go on ahead. Don't worry, I'll call a cab," he said.

Daniel nodded. "Of course, Marc. I'm so sorry. I never thought the school board would mobilize so quickly. I should have anticipated something like this."

"Daniel, how could you know? Usually it takes a year to get on those people's agenda. I'll be okay," he said, pushing him away. "I'll check in with you tomorrow. Maybe Penny and I can catch a ride with you?"

Daniel didn't like their plan to attend the service at Family First Church, but the two of them had worn him down. "Okay. Hey, kid? Hang in there. It's gotta get better. Really."

Thirty-two

Spooner wanted to get out of the hospital as soon as possible. The scene was getting on her nerves. How much longer could she endure being called "Ms. Spooner" or even worse, "Clar-*ri*-ssa?"

Then again, Spooner thought, the sponge bath thing was somewhat intriguing. Other than feeling self-conscious, and a bit as though the nurse and she were being filmed in a porn movie, it was very satisfying. No wonder people played doctor.

Spooner was entertaining this scenario when Penny walked in. "Hey," she said tentatively, "remember me?"

That killed the fantasy right there. "Ms. Iowa," Spooner answered. "The way Marc talked, D2 wasn't letting you out of solitary confinement for nothing."

"He thinks I'm somewhere else," Penny said. "Namely, tucked away in my apartment. Mind if I sit down?" She seemed distracted.

"Go ahead," Spooner said as if she had a choice.

"Thanks," Penny sat, anchoring her short skirt under her long thighs.

"So, I'd imagine that the conference you were in town for was—extended?"

"Busted." Penny smiled self-consciously. "I've never been a good liar. And to be honest, when I met you, I hadn't quite figured out that it was a women's bar."

"You pick up stuff quick," Spooner said. She felt her headache coming back. "By the way, where's Marc?"

Penny looked down. "I don't know. I thought that maybe you did."

Spooner could tell that look of trouble on her face. "Now what's going on?"

"You've seen the photo in the paper? Yeah, you did." Penny read Spooner's face. "Marc and Daniel just visited the principal of his school. Marc was requested to take a leave of absence until the situation has corrected itself. 'The situation,' of course, being me."

"Shit," Spooner said.

"Exactly." Penny inhaled. "I have created a mess for him with his job. I've ruined things for him." She paused for almost a minute. "For Marc's sake," she continued, "I think I need to stay the hell out of his life."

"You don't mean break up with him?" Spooner asked, suddenly aware of the meaning of Penny's words.

Penny stared at the wall.

"Are you fucking crazy?" Spooner yelled. Lowering her voice to a normal level, she continued. "Why do you think he's going through all of this? He is in love with you." After she said it, Spooner realized that not only was it true, but she believed that it was the best fucking thing for her little brother. She immediately wondered how much of a crack over the head she really got.

"Don't you think I know that?" Penny replied. "Because of me, Lenny's dead. Because of me, Marc has lost the one job in the world that he loves. Even if he gets it back, he will never be able to do that job with pure pleasure, with nothing hanging over his head." Penny looked at Spooner with sad brown eyes.

The sponge bath nurse ran in. "Clar-*ri*-ssa, is everything okay?" Then she zeroed in on Penny. "Ma'am, Miss Cla-ri-ssa needs her rest. I don't want you to get her riled up."

"I'm fine," Spooner said. "I'm sorry I yelled just then."

"That's okay," she said, looking at Penny suspiciously, as if she had just caught Penny cutting Spooner's lifeline. "Just call if you need me."

When Sponge Bath Nurse left, Penny said, "I can't risk hurting Marc any more than I've already done. I just can't do it to him, Spooner." Her voice cracked as she fought back tears.

Spooner sighed. "Are you sure you're not a dyke? Sure are sounding like one now. Every lesbian I know has this strange fascination for tragedy. It's almost like we can't sustain the thought of just being happy with someone. It's always 'Oh, it's my fault,' or 'Why don't I break her heart before she can screw up mine because no two people in this world can be as good as we are together?' I don't know what your particular drama preference is. I would suspect the 'I'm responsible for Original Sin' one. But just think about it." Spooner looked her straight in the eyes. "You're in love with him too, right? This is your one chance to love the way you never loved before. The kind of love you hets talk about—to have and to hold, through sickness and health, through floods and badlands, and whatever the hell. One chance. Take it."

Now who was pulling a *General Fucking Hospital* routine? Spooner wondered.

Of course Spooner's little speech made Penny cry even more than before. "Oh, shit," she replied to Penny's tears, "and here I don't have any tissues."

Then Penny spotted the unopened box on Spooner's bed stand. *An extra twenty bucks on my bill*, Spooner calculated. She had not opened the box for more than twenty-four hours, and Penny had gotten to it in ten minutes. "Do we have an understanding?" Spooner asked, hoping to run the kid out before she incurred any more damage to her hospital bill.

Penny nodded. "I'd better get going. Spooner—"

"No, no. Don't thank me. We didn't have this conversation." How fucking melodramatic.

"Actually," Penny replied, "I was going to say that I'll pay for the tissues." She smiled as she took a wad of them out of the box and put them in her purse.

Thirty-three

"Ravenswood, just south of Balmoral," Penny said to the cabdriver.

He turned around. "Not you again."

"Don't worry. This time I do have a destination."

He grunted and pulled away from the hospital toward Marc's place. Penny knew she wasn't supposed to go to Marc's, but he wasn't answering his phone. Penny was worried.

"Wait here," Penny instructed the driver. "I'll be right back."

"Yeah, yeah. My luck."

Marc wasn't there. No answer. No lights. Fortunately for Penny, he had failed to lock the door, so she was able to do a thorough search. "Okay," she said, getting back into the car, "let's go." She rattled off the address of Marc's school, which she had found on a refrigerator magnet. It was in the shape of a ruler.

"I don't do the South Side, lady," he said.

Penny had anticipated this, but was not prepared to argue legalities with him. "An extra twenty's in it for you. You don't even have to stop. You can just slow down and I'll roll out the door."

"You're a funny lady." He was not amused. "Okay, for old times' sake. And if you promise that I'll never see you again."

"Promise," Penny said as they zoomed off.

* * * * * * * * * * *

"Penny, how the hell did you get here?"

"Shhh," Penny replied as she slipped into Marc's darkened classroom. "I told you I wanted to see this." She looked up at the ceiling and saw thousands of tiny stars twinkling back. "This is incredible! Did you do this?"

"How did you get in?" Marc was insistent.

"The custodian let me in. I told him I was a friend of yours." And anticipating her next question, Penny showed him the magnet with the address. "You really should lock your door." She paused. "I was getting worried about you."

Penny touched Marc's face. Tears. "Sweetie, I'm sorry about all this. Daniel told me. I've not only made a colossal mess for myself, I've also ruined this for you."

"Pen, how could you possibly know this was going to happen? Anyway, the picture is my fault. I was the one that answered the door without looking out the spy hole. And after all, you did warn me that your life was—what did you say? You know, the morning after?"

"I believe I said that my life was somewhat conflicted." Penny sighed. "Quite an understatement, if you ask me."

"That it is," he said. "But as crazy as it is, I love you."

"But Marc—"

"It'll be okay," he said.

They stood silently for a long time. Minutes. Then Marc took her hand. Penny's eyes had adjusted to the darkness; the pinpricks of light above gave her enough light to see that half of the classroom was arranged like a theater in the round, with the middle section lower than the rest. In the middle of the room was a large machine. Penny assumed that this was the origination of the star show. Marc had somehow transformed a classroom into a planetarium. The other side was arranged like a typical classroom.

"What the—" Marc said, picking a piece of paper off the floor. "Oh my God."

"What?" Penny asked.

"I had forgotten about something that happened last Friday. It was one of my students. Her name is Fiona. She's one of my favorites—not that I'm supposed to have favorites. But she was distracted, edgy. Something was wrong. I thought it had to do with Disney World and The Hulk."

"What, Marc?" Penny waited for more, but only silence filled the gap. "I don't know what you're saying, sweetie."

"I don't know what I'm saying either. Shield your eyes," Marc said as he turned on a small desk lamp. He quickly read the note, then handed it to Penny. "A student of mine, Fiona Clarke, dropped this when she left on Friday. She was about to say something, but her mother came to get her, so she couldn't finish. I think she wrote this note just in case—"

Penny unfolded a piece of spiral-bound notebook paper. The mere act of unfolding it took her immediately back to her own childhood and the dozens of notes she had written to friends. She expected to see a question like, "Do you like Harry? Circle Yes or No."

Instead she found an earnest note from a student to her teacher. Fiona's handwriting was tentative, with slanted strokes that suggested she was a lefty:

Dear Doctor H:

I'm not sure how to say this to your, so I writing it just in case I chicken out. I think somethnigs going to happen to you that will send you away from school. I cant tell you why or how I know this, but I can feel it. And a door and a picture, thats the worse part. Stay away from a man with a camra. Hes going to ruin it all for you. You have been my favorite teacher, and I dont want to lose you, even though the Hulk says your gay and just need a good woman to straighten you out.

Fiona C.

P.S. I keep thinking that you should stay away from that woman, but I don't think you'll be able to. It's like density or something.

Penny stared at Marc. "Your student wrote this?"

Marc nodded. "She dropped it when she left. I was going to pick it up, but …" He paused in remembrance. "When she left, she said, 'You have been a great teacher.' I thought the past tense was a bit odd, but then I forgot all about the note. Fiona knew. She predicted it all."

"How were you to know that one of your students is psychic? You couldn't know that, Marc." Penny leaned over and kissed him. "It was me, not you, who set the sequence in motion. I was the woman, after all. Let it go, Marc, let it go." She whispered the words. Her voice caressed his ear, prompting an unexpected emotion.

"Come. Watch your step," he said, leading Penny down steps to the center of the room. Silently they reached the bottom. Marc lingered on the last step, giving him six extra inches; he pulled Penny close and kissed her gently. A soft sigh escaped Penny's lips, surprising both of them into laughter.

Marc pulled Penny down to the floor. "I am so in love with you. It's crazy, I know." He lay next to her, lightly touching her face, tracing his finger down to her breasts, down her hips, thighs, tracing with his touch through the fabric of her clothes until she ached with desire.

Penny worked to reach out to him, but Marc held her off. "Enjoy your body," he whispered. "I certainly am." He teased Penny without roaming under her clothes.

Marc was surprised by the intensity of his desire and slowly removed his own shirt. He made his fingers work slowly, teasingly, with the deliberate movement of each finger unhooking each button on his shirt and moving to the next one. Penny looked at Marc's chest, shadowed and highlighted all at once by the stars above. Before she could stop herself, she kissed Marc urgently, pulling at his jeans.

Penny noticed and did not notice Marc doing the same to her.

They straddled each other, touching deeply, trying to give and feel pleasure, transported to a place where touch and love pulsed in one delicious rhythm, burned and caressed by the gentle piercing lights above. A place where murder and scandal wouldn't touch them, if only for a moment.

Marc felt the weight of desire, shocking him into awareness of her body's pleasure. He shouldn't have been surprised. "Density" pulled them together.

Thirty-four

Benjamin Lane spotted Boots as soon as she walked into the warehouse-sized auditorium. "I'm glad you came, Officer," he said, pumping her hand. This time she didn't correct him.

Normally Boots kept a respectable distance between herself and suspects. This was difficult in the case of Benjamin Lane. On the one hand, she did not want to encourage a false sense of relationship. Yet, as with the case with Minnie and Gerry Rantzhoff, she knew there was a lot Benjamin wasn't saying about Lenny Blue.

"I don't want to disturb you," Boots said. "I see from the bulletin you're preaching for the service."

"Lenny would have liked it that way." Benjamin nodded sincerely. "Did sis tell you how 'close' he and I were?"

"No, she didn't," Boots said, knowing that even if she did, it was none of his damn business. "I might have some more questions later. Will you be available?"

"Sure, Officer. How about dinner?"

Again with the officer stuff. "Right now, I think that we'd better keep things professional." Boots knew she had made a mistake the moment she said it.

"Oh, I get it," he whispered back conspiratorially. "Well, I'll see you onstage." He winked as he walked away.

"You vixen!" Daniel whispered as he came up behind her.

"D2, you scared the hell out of me." Boots was embarrassed by how the whole scene looked. Avoiding the subject altogether, she asked, "Where's your client, I mean, Ms. Lane? I also need to meet Mr. Davis, if he's here."

"Oh, they're here," Daniel answered. "They're slightly disguised. We thought that with the publicity, they'd be better off if they blended into the woodwork a little bit. Though I'm not all that happy we're here in the first place."

"That's understandable," Boots said. "I guess you weren't one of the first five hundred, eh? No commemorative picture of the deceased?"

Daniel grunted. "You'd think this was Wrigley Field or some damn thing," he said, referring to the ballpark for the Chicago Cubs. "This place is creepy. Everyone is sad, sure, but the mood is, what? Almost joyous at the same time."

Boots shrugged. "People think Mr. Blue is in a better place now. I guess some folks see death as a time of celebration. But I have to agree with you. This place is definitely creepy. I would like to see where Ms. Lane was standing Sunday night."

"Okay," he said. "I'll go get her. Stay here."

Boots was trying to estimate the seating capacity of the auditorium when a little old lady approached her. "Looking for someone, honey?"

"Well, I was waiting for someone—Ms. Lane?" Boots whispered the last words of her sentence.

"You found her," the false old lady replied. The disguise was complete. Penny had been transformed into Mrs. Doubtfire.

"Would you show me where you were standing on Sunday evening?" Boots asked.

"Sure, but why?" Penny led the way.

"It helps me to recreate the scene," Boots lied. She couldn't tell her the bad news that her brother had blown her alibi.

Penny took her to the back of the sanctuary, near the exit closest to the parking lot. "I waited in this aisle at about here," she said.

"This is quite a distance," Boots said, wondering why Penny ever thought her brother would be able to recognize her from the podium. "Ms. Lane, how many people does this place hold?"

"Fifteen hundred. There's an overflow room that seats five hundred more. They're expecting at least that many for this thing." She stopped. "I'd better get back and sit down. Do you want us to save you a seat?"

"I'm going to wander around." Boots knew she couldn't sit in one place without feeling trapped. "But would all of you wait for me across the street at Moonstone's after this is over? I'd like to check in with you before we go to the funeral."

"The real service," Penny added, referring to the private funeral she had helped the Rantzhoffs plan. "I have a feeling that this is going to be more like a circus than a memorial service."

Boots sat down in the back on the opposite side of the church, away from where Penny had stood and out of Benjamin's sight. It was the only seat available in that row. "Whew," she said to no one in particular and everyone around her, "it's warm in here." Boots unzipped her mock-turtleneck yellow jacket. Underneath the jacket she wore an embroidered multicolored vest with a black shirt.

"No wonder you were warm," the young woman sitting on Boots' right commented. She was using her commemorative picture as a fan. "You know," she whispered, "I panicked a little when you took off the jacket. I didn't know if you had anything on underneath it."

My point exactly, Boots thought as she continued her alterations. "With April coming, you just never know how to dress. In fact, I am still warm. You wouldn't happen to know how to French-braid hair, would you?"

"Do I? Of course. It's one of my favorite things to do in the world." Without noticing the visible cues of annoyance around them, the woman set down the glossy photo of Lenny and grabbed Boots's long black hair. The braid finally settled at the middle of Boots's back. (Out of frustration, an emotional duet of women directly behind them found different seats. They were here to say good-bye to Lenny Blue, and not to watch the drama directly in front of them.)

Two minutes after Boots's hair was coiffed, the sanctuary grew dark. Then, on a large screen, the audience saw video clips from Lenny's life. Several smaller TV screens flipped down as well above their heads; these gave a clearer view of the large screen. Some childhood pictures were used, but mostly concert footage and professional music videos. During most of the video clips, the audience sang along. Boots heard lots of sniffling. The woman who had braided her hair confessed, "Lenny was like the John Lennon of the group. Deep, passionate, misunderstood, tragic. I can't believe he just performed here last Friday and now he's gone. Just like Gareth Grace," she added. "God, I was in love with him," she said, trailing into tears.

Gareth Grace? Boots wondered. Who was that?

Boots was so distracted by the amount of grief that consumed the crowd around her that she almost missed the significance of what flicked across the dozens of screens. But when she saw it, she suddenly realized all was not well.

This clip was not slick, not professional. It was taken by a single home video camera. She got a sick feeling in her stomach.

"You are my fans," said a very alive Lenny. "And I love you all. You have been supportive, loving, kind. I have enjoyed your energy, your affection, your letters of support."

No wonder folks were in love with him, Boots realized. His voice seduced them.

Boots patted the grieving woman on the arm, "I'll be back," she said as if the woman cared. She kept her eyes on the screen as she moved quickly from her seat, stepping on a few feet before she was freed from that row.

The videotape continued to roll. "And I believe we'll all meet in heaven." Lenny's tenor voice was lyrical, mesmerizing. "God's will is His will. Romans 5:21: 'That as sin hath reigned unto death, even so might grace reign through righteousness unto eternal life—'"

The more Boots saw, the more she was convinced they were watching Lenny's Last Will and Testament. She noticed another disturbing aspect.

He was wearing Penny's red leather jacket. The one later found in the Dumpster, covered with blood.

Boots ran out into the foyer and accosted an usher preparing for the offering. Flashing her wallet, a habit from her cop years, Boots asked, "Where is the video room?"

He pointed to the balcony, and she took the stairs two steps at a time. She burst into the room and scared the video man to death.

This time she stopped herself from flashing her badgeless wallet. *"Stop that video right now and hand it over."*

She heard Lenny's voice echo from everywhere: "And as the writer of Ecclesiastes says, 'Vanity of vanities, all is vanity. What profit has a man of all his labour which he taketh under the sun? One generation passeth away, and another generation cometh; but the earth abides for ever … That which is crooked cannot be made straight: and that which is wanting cannot be numbered—'"

He looked around, expecting the backups any moment. "But—"

"*I said stop the video and hand it over.* It is evidence in a police investigation." Boots was sweating. That tape needed to end before two thousand people became witnesses to their hero's death. *"Now."*

"Shit," he said, nervously hitting buttons until the tape stopped. He handed it to her.

"Who gave you that tape?" she asked.

"No one. I mean, it was just sitting here with the rest." He looked as if he might drop dead on sight.

She softened her voice. "Rerun some of those other videos. Just the ones already shown, though." She reviewed the stack of tapes for any other surprises. The others looked innocent. "If anyone asks you about what just happened, tell them to talk to me." Boots handed him one of her business cards.

He nodded, and put it in his pocket; then he found another tape and slipped it into the machine.

Boots relaxed. "You've been very cooperative. Thank you." She hid the videotape between her shirt and vest, hoping that perspiration wouldn't damage it. She ran back down the steps and found the usher in the same place she had left him. "Where's the pay phone?" she asked, cursing herself for leaving her cell phone in the car. He pointed around the corner.

Boots dialed quickly. "Jimmy, I've got something big here. Meet me across the street from Family First Church at Moonstone's. As soon as you can get up here."

Boots had one more thing she needed to do. Sensing that the video show was nearly over, she slipped back into the sanctuary, this time on the side where Penny had stood just Sunday evening.

She only had to wait a few minutes. When the lights came up, there was Benjamin Lane at the podium. As Boots watched him nervously scan the audience, she saw his eyes stop on her. And when she looked up at the TV camera just above her head, Boots saw him open his eyes a little larger, then smile. He had recognized her. He did not recognize her because of her clothing or her hair, as she had changed those since the service began. He recognized Boots's face.

The hell he couldn't see Penny, Boots realized as she tipped her hand toward him, then left the sanctuary the moment his eyes left her.

Thirty-five

Boots hadn't been the only one to miss the sermon. Daniel, Marc, Penny, and Gary waited at the corner across the street from Family First Church, pretending to be catching a bus, as there was no sign of a Moonstone Coffee and Tea.

Boots joined them, scratching her head. "I could have sworn I saw a Moonstone's over here. Or maybe it used to be here. I'm sorry about that. You must be Mr. Davis," she said as she introduced herself to Gary.

"Quite a show, huh?" said Gary. "How the hell did Benny orchestrate that?"

Penny was silent. Her pale complexion mirrored her thoughts.

"You okay?" Boots asked her, guessing Penny saw the jacket. "You know, let's wait to talk about this," Boots added, seeing James Bay walking down the street with a perplexed look on his face. "Bus stop's over here," she yelled to him.

"There's no Moonstone here," he said to her when he got closer.

"We've established that," Boots agreed, and she introduced him to the others. "Jimmy, I need to talk with you a second. Let's walk to the car. Will you folks wait a little longer?"

Assuming they said yes, she started walking.. "I have a videotape here that I want you to take to the station. Hand it over to Bryson. I haven't seen it all, but you guys look it over. See if there is any way to date it."

"Sure," he said. "By the way, Bryson wants to bring Steale in again. On account of the jacket. He didn't like her answer yesterday. I can't say that I blame him. How does someone lose something like that?"

"Stall him," Boots said, realizing that the videotape might make Penny's interrogation even more desirable. "I have a feeling that something's about to bust. Ms. Lane—Ms. Steale is in good hands with her lawyer. She won't be skipping town or anything. It's Benjamin Lane I'm worried about. I don't want us to lose track of him. What about the autopsy yesterday?"

Jimmy shrugged. "His heart stopped."

Everyone's heart stops when you die. "You're not just shitting me, are you?" Boots asked.

"For once, no. The kid did have a seizure, or maybe several. That much Bridge did find out. There's some damage to the heart, though she's not convinced that any of this would be abnormal if the person hit the kid in the right spot on the noggin. She's still trying to puzzle it out. And of course drugs are always a possibility. There's some screwy stuff with the blood work. The lab misplaced it for a day, so they're working at it this afternoon. We'll get some of the results soon." He checked his watch. "I'd better get going. I'll let you know the second I know anything." Jimmy waved the tape and moved to his car.

As Boots returned to the bus stop, she knew they hadn't waited to talk about the video; she heard Gary just say "Thank God the tape broke. Who knows what Lenny was leading up to?"

"Mr. Davis, I've been thinking," Boots said, pretending to be oblivious of their conversation, "that maybe on the way to the service you should ride with me."

"Uh, sure," Gary said, giving a wary eye toward Penny, then Daniel. "Meet you guys there?"

There was an exchange of some type of signal between Gary and Daniel, but Boots was unable to read it. "My car's over here," she said.

* * * * * * * * * *

A subdued mood blanketed Penny, Marc, and Daniel as they traveled to Lenny's private service. Daniel's thoughts centered on two questions. First: Why had Boots decided to interrogate Gary now? Did she know something that Daniel didn't? Did she suspect something that Daniel didn't want to admit to himself?

Then it hit him. He had been sloppy again.

On Monday, Gary had visited Benjamin after he learned about Lenny's death. Penny had found Gary only after calling Benjamin and locating Gary there. Yet Gary despised Benjamin Lane. Why would Gary visit Benjamin rather than call Penny? Daniel had assumed that the reason stemmed from compromising Daniel's position with Penny. Suddenly he wasn't all that sure.

There was no way that Gary staged Lenny's death. They had been together all evening. But was Gary more involved in Lenny's death than Daniel wanted to believe? As an accomplice?

Daniel told himself to stop jumping to conclusions.

Daniel's second concern was just as hard to let go, since it was the question Penny raised as soon as they got into the car.

"How did Lenny get my jacket?" Penny wondered as she hurried to shed her persona as an old woman

She asked that question several times before anyone responded. Daniel saw the question led nowhere and changed the subject. "If—" he started, looking at her in the rearview mirror. "If you were to guess how recent that video was, what would you say?"

"Pretty recent," she said. "He had lost weight in the last few months. I'd say that it was filmed since the Grammys."

"How about as recent as this weekend? Since you'd lost the jacket?" Daniel probed.

Marc saw where that question was leading. He gave Daniel a sidelong glance from the front seat. "D2, are you suggesting that he taped this in anticipation of his death? As if he knew that he was going to die?"

"Or commit suicide?" Penny asked.

"But he didn't kill himself," Marc said. "It was just staged like that."

Something wasn't fitting here. "What about those words he was quoting?" Daniel asked. "I'd assume that they were Bible verses, right, Penny?"

"Yeah," she replied. "I'm not the best authority on religion, but Lenny's selections seemed off somehow. I mean, if I were going to use a video as a retrospective of my life, I would have picked different types of verses. Ones that seemed to draw meaning out of my life, or at least would comfort other people."

"Like Psalm 23 or something?" Daniel asked, remembering only about that much from his Lutheran church upbringing.

"Yeah, or like the Paul passage about running the race well, and getting a crown of glory and all that stuff," Penny said. "Now I've exhausted my Bible knowledge."

"Who's Paul?" Marc asked. "But again, that's assuming that this was a suicide tape or something. It's not."

Daniel wasn't done with his questions. "Marc, let's put aside speculation about Lenny's motive right now. I don't think we'll be able to determine that until all the pieces are here." He slowed his speed; he didn't need a ticket on the way to the funeral. "Did anyone else hear that thing about not making the crooked path straight? Do you think he was saying something there?"

"D2, I don't follow—oh," Marc said, "you mean, straight as in not gay?"

Penny sat up. "If he did commit suicide—no, Marc, hear me out." She held her hand up to hold off Marc's objection. "If he did commit suicide, maybe he wanted it to look like it was because of lost love. Not because he was struggling with homosexuality. But since that was the real issue, he inadvertently left the clues of that in the tape too."

Daniel shook his head. "Penny, I have to agree with Marc. It doesn't make sense. First of all, he didn't commit suicide. The police wouldn't reclassify the death if Lenny had killed himself. Second, why would he do this? No one was—" Daniel almost said, no one was putting a gun to his head. He continued. "Who would have been condemning him? He had ended things with Gary once you two were engaged. Why would he have done this?"

"Because he had to. Because it was God's will," Penny whispered. "That's what Lenny said when I broke up with him," she explained. "I had just told him that I didn't love him like a wife should love a husband, and he told me that he knew that, but we had to get married anyway. Maybe he proposed in the first place because he thought heterosexuality was God's will."

"So you're saying Lenny believed that he was trying to cure being gay by marrying you? Why would he think something like that? Who would have been feeding him that kind of line?" Daniel asked, turning around to look at her.

She smiled weakly. "I guess there is one more thing I forgot to tell you about my brother. Have you ever heard of Leviticus Incorporated?"

"You mean, the ex-gay group?"

Penny nodded sadly. "Benjamin Lane is a founding member."

Daniel almost ran off the road.

Thirty-six

"Mr. Davis, does the name Gareth Grace ring a bell for you?" Boots asked as they walked to her car.

It was not quite the question Gary expected. "Vaguely. He was a Christian rocker in the late eighties. I think he died in an anti abortion protest, heart attack or something. Benjamin liked him a lot."

"Hmmm," Boots said. "Someone at the service mentioned Lenny Blue, John Lennon, and Gareth Grace in the same breath. I was just wondering what the connection was."

As she drove them to Hyde Park, she asked Gary about his activities leading up to last Sunday evening. He told her he had stayed at a friend's house the night before and left about two in the afternoon. He then stopped at home, gotten the call from Penny, then visited her from roughly three to four o'clock. After that he returned home to get ready for a date and spent the evening at the date's house. Boots assumed from the vague language he used to describe his "friend" and "date" that Gary was seeing a man.

Though Boots wanted to question him further about the events leading to Lenny's death, she switched to inquire about his impression of the video. Boots was sure she missed some key facial responses since she was driving. Even so, Gary's voice was textured with nuance.

"I still don't get that stunt," he said. "I don't know what the hell Benjamin was thinking about with that. It was like a 3-D suicide note."

"Do you really think Mr. Lane okayed that?" asked Boots.

"I'm positive he did," Gary replied. "How else would something like that end up on the screen? And if we had stayed for his sermon, I bet we'd have heard every single Bible passage Lenny mentioned woven in."

"Were Mr. Lane and Mr. Rantzhoff close?"

"Benjamin and Lenny? Not really, at least not at first. Ben was amazed at Lenny's popularity after the Grammys. He was grooming Len for a solo album and was pulling together video clips for the project, hence the little light show we saw back there. I don't even think Penny knew about that," Gary said.

"Were you and Mr. Rantzhoff close?"

A pause. "Yes," he sighed. "And I might as well get this out of the way. We had been, uh, together, before his engagement to Penny."

Boots had already figured this one out. Gary now placed himself squarely in the suspect category: under the "spurned lover" heading. "And did anyone know about this? Except for the two of you?" Boots questioned.

"No, at least not during the relationship. And well, I tried to keep any of my personal business as far away from Benjamin as possible." Gary's voice was thick with dislike for Benjamin Lane.

"I know that Mr. Lane is, well, shall we say, not very tolerant of homosexuality," Boots said.

"Are you kidding?" Gary said. "How could he be? He is one of the success stories of the ex-gay ministry world. He's got quite a testimony," he added, voice dripping with sarcasm.

Thirty-seven

Penny stood at the doorway of the church with Gerald and Minnie Rantzhoff; somewhere along the way she had lost her Mrs. Doubtfire disguise. Boots was still perplexed by her interview with Minnie on Monday and had more questions. This was obviously not the right time. Questions could wait until after the funeral.

Penny greeted Boots and Gary, passing them along to Lenny's parents. "I'm sorry about your loss," Boots said. Unimaginative words that came automatically with the job, she realized as she took a few steps into the church. Gary hugged each of them.

"Gary, we haven't seen you around much the last few months," Mr. Rantzhoff said, a husky, no-nonsense man with the build of a football player rather than a music professor.

"Uh, well," Gary stumbled. "With the wedding plans, you know, I didn't want to get in the way."

Boots and Gary moved into the sanctuary. A closed casket drowned in white flowers dominated her attention. As usual, no one paid much attention to the "no flowers" request of the family. With only a few minutes to spare before the service, a few dozen mourners dotted the long wooden pews. Boots doubted a whole lot of people were invited, and would bet her life that no one would be offered a prize for attendance. She watched Gary take a seat next to Marc.

"Where's D2?" Boots asked Marc.

"Outside," he mouthed.

He wasn't outside. Boots found him in what appeared to be a basement room that, before Illinois's ban on smoking, was likely a smokers' lounge. *Strange thing to have in a church,* she thought as she came up behind him. He was lighting up.

"You didn't tell me practically the whole damn band was queer," Boots said quietly.

"Just found out myself," Daniel responded. "Faggot?" he asked, pointing the pack of cigarettes at her.

She took a cigarette; he lit it. "I hate smoking," Boots said, secretly grateful for the lit tobacco, which immediately did its magic on her frayed nerves.

"Me too," Daniel said, coughing like a neophyte.

* * * * * * * * * *

Mr. and Mrs. Rantzhoff invited Gary to sit in the front pew next to them and Penny. Daniel joined Marc a row behind them. Boots took a seat with John Bryson in the back of the sanctuary.

"I heard it was quite a show," Bryson whispered to Boots.

"I couldn't even begin to tell you. Did Jimmy fill you in?"

"Oh yeah. He's watching Lane as we speak." Benjamin Lane was not present at this service. Gary had told Boots he had not been invited. Boots found that unsurprising, but telling nonetheless.

After the typical Protestant opening prayers and readings, the parents stood near their son's coffin. Mr. Rantzhoff spoke, with his wife standing at his side. "We looked through Lenny's music journals to find an appropriate song for today, something that would give us hope about the healing of grief. But we kept returning to the one we decided to sing for you today, which is really not very hopeful. But it's honest." His voice cracked. "It's actually one of Lenny's first songs. He wrote it when he was a teenager."

They sang the song a cappella to a familiar tune:

> Love splits the heart apart
> Hate tears it even more
> Both created from the start
> Desire and pain, the bond.

The poem was a thinly veiled cry, one that was probably buried in the depths of Lenny's journal. And judging by the faces of the grieving parents, they understood their son's pathos.

Then Boots figured out the tune. "Blest Be the Tie That Binds." How ironic.

There was obviously more, but the parents couldn't finish. Minnie Rantzhoff stepped down first. Gerry Rantzhoff opened his mouth as if to speak, then closed it and followed his wife off the stage. Penny moved to sit between them, with arms around their shoulders.

Boots looked over the small gathering. Most wiped tears away from their eyes. A few, Gary included, fought it; Boots could tell by his rigid body. When reality finally hit him, it would be ten times worse, she predicted to no one but herself. She'd seen it happen many times. It had happened to her.

A few silent minutes passed. A man who looked vaguely familiar, who had been sitting by a woman also vaguely familiar, stood. He greeted both parents with a clasped hand, and stepped up to the podium. *Here it comes, the saccharine sermon, diminishing all the harsh realities of Lenny's life and uplifting the hope one can find in heaven*, Boots predicted.

She couldn't have been more wrong. Terry Jones was both the pastor of this church—Peace Congregational—and a volunteer for Blue Vista Youth Club, a resource center for teens who wished to explore their gay or lesbian sexuality in a supportive, healthy environment. Apparently Lenny had spent time a few years ago as a volunteer at Blue Vista. He apparently quit when the band took to the road.

No wonder he looked familiar to Boots. Jones had been the master of ceremonies for the Blue Vista Ball just last Friday—the one at which Boots had made a token appearance.

Jones talked openly about Lenny's sexuality. "We are not sure what happened with Lenny, why he would undo all the good work he had done to be all he was," Pastor Jones concluded. "But until we foster a society that allows the full expression of all people—no matter their skin color, their gender, their sexual attractions, their religious foundations—we will never be free. And to all those who quote the Bible to condemn homosexuality, I say right back, 'Woe to them who preach evil, and proclaim it to be good.' It is evil to allow the destruction of a human being because he or she can never be heterosexual. It is not good."

Terry Jones ended his words and returned to his pew with the familiar woman, whom Boots now remembered was his wife, Dale Sentry. Dale also happened to be Marc's ex-lover.

Apparently Marc was so preoccupied that he had not even noticed that particular ex in the room.

It was obvious to Boots that Dale zeroed in on Marc.

As Spooner would say, *General Fucking Hospital.*

Boots was so caught up with this particular drama unfolding that she had no idea how long Daniel had been signaling to her. Bryson finally nudged her attention in Daniel's direction. Daniel looked wide-eyed as he mouthed, "Obituary." Once she deciphered his words, she understood what had seemed odd to her last Monday.

The *Tribune* obituary directed donations in Lenny's memory to be given to Blue Youth Scholarship. Boots had assumed the Rantzhoffs were setting up a scholarship fund in honor of their son, whose stage name was Lenny Blue. What they really were asking for were donations to the Blue *Vista* Youth Scholarship, a full-tuition award given annually to an outstanding Chicago gay or lesbian youth. Maybe the newspaper had gotten it wrong. Then again, maybe it hadn't.

It was also crystal clear why Lenny chose "Blue" for his stage name. When he had started with the band, he had been working closely with Blue Vista.

Boots had not asked Minnie the right questions on Monday. Minnie Rantzhoff knew all along that their son was gay. And Boots would bet that Gerald Rantzhoff did as well.

Bryson checked his phone; he showed Boots the text message: "Have Boots call me ASAP." As soon as the final prayers began, she slid out into the lobby and used the pay phone, again cursing that she forgot her cell phone.

"The verdict's in," he said, referring to the official ruling on Lenny Blue's cause of death.

"Well?" Boots asked.

"Guess." Jimmy was in a playful mood.

Boots was not. "James, this is not a good time."

"Just guess."

"I never saw the body at the scene of the crime. But I'd guess a blow to the head. Something that someone wanted to cover with a gun wound."

"Nope." His voice was smiling, smug. Jimmy loved it when Boots was wrong. "Phenothiazine sudden death. Basically, the kid convulsed and asphyxiated." He paraphrased the rest: "Then his heart went nuts and eventually conked out."

Boots surmised from Jimmy's description that drugs were involved. "What did they find in his system?"

"The kid died from Thorazine overdose."

Thorazine? "What is it? And where the hell would someone get a hold of something like that?"

Jimmy had asked the toxicologist that same question. "Someone with a psychotic or bipolar condition would have a prescription for it. All we need to do is to find that someone and we'll probably find a hell of a lot of their medication gone."

"Good God!" she said as the cruelty of Lenny's death washed over her. Whoever killed Lenny must have been ignorant of the results of this drug, or a sadist.

Jimmy continued. "You're gonna hate this next part, though. The ME says that the OD looks like a suicide to her."

"What? Someone staged a suicide to cover a suicide? That is the screwiest thing I have ever heard of."

"Oh, it's screwy all right," he replied. "The kid's autopsy profiles like a suicide—except for the shooting at the end, of course. And I'd have to agree with her. I think you'd agree too, once you saw the whole tape—"

Minnie Rantzhoff had said that her son had dealt with depression. Could he have taken his own life? Boots heard the organ signal the final hymn. "Shit," she said, forgetting her resolve not to curse in church. "I've got to get going. Bryson's here. He told me you're tailing Lane."

"Did he tell you about the tape?" He read her silence as a no. "Well, just ask him about it. Lane's still at Family First. When he leaves, I'll roll with him."

Boots had barely gotten off the phone with Jimmy when she felt a tap on her shoulder. She turned around.

"Penny asked me to give you this," Marc said as he handed her a folded note.

Boots took a step away as she read the message.

I think I know where Lenny's video was filmed.

Boots wasn't sure if she could handle any more revelations.

Thirty-eight

"It's good to see you again, Officer," Benjamin Lane said as he opened the door. He was holding a cup of coffee. "Though I was afraid that I had 'lost' you yesterday at the service."

"I won't take much of your time. I just need to ask you a few questions." Boots walked through the opened door and accidentally brushed against Benjamin's belly.

"I'm still a suspect?" he asked as he countered his excitement over the lady cop's "accidental" brush against his body.

What an odd question, Boots noted. And what did he mean by "still"? "You know," she said, "I was surprised that you could see me from that back aisle yesterday. I mean, it was so far away."

"Well," he said, moving them into the living room, "I would like to say that it's because of my 'eagle' eyesight, but I can't take all the credit. You see, not only can the audience see me close up on those television monitors—I can see the audience by looking at monitors built into the podium. That way, we can tell if we're 'reaching' people with our sermons. You just happened to be standing right by a camera. I could see your face as clear as right now."

"Fascinating," Boots said. "I have to say it. Yesterday was quite a show. It was like Lenny was right there."

"It was amazing, wasn't it?" he agreed. "I don't know where that tape came from, but it fit perfectly into my sermon."

"I mean, it was like he was still alive," Boots prodded.

"Though I'm not sure why he chose to wear that jacket. It made him look ridiculous. Of course it's ruined beyond repair now," Benjamin said with regret, not realizing he had just made her job easier.

"It's funny you say that, Mr. Lane, because the only people that knew about the demise of that jacket are members of the Chicago police."

His face got whiter than it already was as he realized his slip.

"How much coffee do you drink a day, Mr. Lane?" Boots asked him.

"Coffee?" he responded, off balance. "Three, maybe four cups a day?"

"Well, you mentioned that you had just picked up a bag from Moonstone's across the street from the church before your sermon on Sunday evening. Incidentally, there is no Moonstone across the street from the church. Then, when I visited you on Tuesday, you mentioned that you just got another bag on Monday, not on Sunday. Unless you drink a lot of coffee, I would say that you were covering up something. You never left to pick up coffee before your sermon, did you? I am thinking that maybe you did leave after it. Maybe to make a delivery to the South Side?"

He knew that Boots was closing in on him. "I didn't kill Lenny Blue."

"Did you know that Mr. Blue had rented an apartment across the way from your sister shortly after their engagement?" Boots continued.

He was silent.

"I think you did. I think that you put him up to it." Boots saw Jimmy peek in through the window in the kitchen door.

She continued. "Mrs. Rantzhoff found an extra set of keys in their washing machine. They figured that Lenny had forgotten to empty his pockets before his last load of laundry. We were all quite surprised to find out that these were keys to another apartment, which he had rented a few months ago. We found a video camera, pointed at what we believe had been the dark drapes Mr. Blue had hung in his windows. We believe these are the same drapes your sister identified as having hung in the windows opposite her bedroom window up until Sunday. Then they were used to 'hide' a red leather jacket in a certain Dumpster on the South Side." Boots couldn't resist the finger quotations.

Boots was relentless. "We also found a lot of pornography on the walls—all of women. And as strange as it may seem, these photos were interspersed with Bible verses naming various biblical couples, heterosexual, of course. And ironically, some of the verses were ones Mr. Blue quoted in his video suicide note."

"So, Lenny had a sexual problem. What does this have to do with me?" Benjamin Lane sat down heavily.

"We also located some of Mr. Blue's journals he kept in the storage locker at this apartment. Ah," she wondered, "I bet you didn't know about the journals. It's really too bad. Those journals go back for almost a year and tell all about you encouraging Mr. Blue's cure from homosexuality, including your suggestion for him to marry your sister. You gave him a tacit blessing to do whatever he needed to do to get the job done, including voyeurism."

"This is crazy," he said. "This is all conjecture."

"I'm afraid it's more than that. The police have all the evidence they need. They also have a search warrant for your home, and for your car. I'm sure they will find even more. I hope you don't mind taking a trip to the station. There are just a few questions they need to ask you," Boots said, signaling Jimmy to come through the door. "You don't mind if I ask a friend to join us, do you? His name is James Bay, and unlike me, he really is a police officer."

"This is coercion," he said. "None of this will stand up in court …" His voice trailed as Jimmy escorted him to a waiting squad car.

Thirty-nine

Benjamin Lane refused to talk unless Penny was in the room as well. And since Daniel was in court that afternoon, Penny asked Boots to join her in the room. With Jimmy and Bryson in there too, the interrogation room was quite crowded.

Benjamin cooperated only because Lenny Blue's cause of death was ruled as a suicide. With that, and the videotape as a clear documentary of Lenny's suicidal intent, no criminal court would ever convict Benjamin Lane of murder. It was still unclear what charges he would face, if any. Benjamin hoped his cooperation would offset any legal ramifications. He refused the counsel of a lawyer because in his eyes, he hadn't done anything wrong.

"You understand that your words will stand in court, should this end up there," John Bryson warned him as Penny and Boots entered the room.

He nodded. "I understand." The light emphasized his fatigue. He had dispensed with the annoying quotations he made with his fingers.

"Benjamin, why?" Penny asked.

"Ms. Lane—" Bryson cautioned.

"No, Officer," Benjamin said. "She deserves some explanation." He turned to his sister. "I know that you don't understand it, but Lenny was really coming around. I mean, look at him. When he started the band, he was an introverted, introspective kid. Then, look at the last review. He was a show stealer. And you know why that was?"

"Maybe because he wasn't treating his bipolar disorder?" Penny asked, still shaken by Lenny's hidden condition.

"It was because of the Lord," Benjamin said. "It was because Len had finally given up his homosexuality, and was serving the Lord. And He was blessing Lenny for his commitment. He was blessing the band too."

Obviously, he hadn't quite given up his homosexuality. According to the autopsy results, Lenny Blue had had sex within hours of his death, and it wasn't with a woman. But neither Penny nor Benjamin needed to know that. "Mr. Lane," Jimmy interjected, "I'm sure you've worked out a nice little spin on this, but maybe we should limit our comments to the day of Mr. Rantzhoff's death. That is what we're trying to ascertain."

"Sure. Of course." He looked at the wall. "Lenny came over Sunday afternoon, like I said. He looked like hell, if you pardon my expression. I assumed that it was because of sis and her decision to date a black man—"

"Please, Mr. Lane, keep to the issue at hand." Even Jimmy was losing patience.

"Well, it's true, isn't it, sis?"

Penny shook her head sadly.

"Well, anyway," Benjamin continued, "he told me that after sis broke up with him he slipped in his walk with the Lord and got drunk. After he caught sis here with, well, you know, Lenny called the press."

Benjamin looked up at the ceiling for inspiration. "Lenny realized that notifying the press was a stupid thing to do but didn't know how to undo it. He had been up all night because of it. I told him to go sleep it off, that I would clean up the mess like always. Like I said before, Lenny took a cab back downtown. He left my place around three thirty Sunday afternoon."

Boots had confirmed the cab trip between Benjamin Lane's home and Lenny's downtown apartment. The cabdriver remembered Mr. Blue had taken a lot of medication during that final trip home, indicating the beginning of the end for Lenny. They even recovered an empty prescription bottle pushed between the seats of the cab. "Then?" Boots prodded.

"Well, I was worried about him. And you too, sis," Benjamin added, talking to Penny. "Since I couldn't do much for either of you at home, I decided to come talk with you in person. I was able to park in the underground garage in Lenny's spot, since Lenny's car wasn't in the space. I assumed he had left it at whatever bar he had gone to the night before. Then I tried to get to see you, but the security guard was a new guy and he wouldn't let me in your building. That was around four. I figured you were under siege since there was the crowd of press outside the building and wouldn't be going anywhere soon. You surprised me by coming out, and then I made those statements. Believe me," he said to his sister, "I would never have said anything if I knew Lenny had been dead."

Bryson interrupted him. "So you didn't go to Mr. Blue's apartment until after your sister left." He had already confirmed this part of his alibi, but he asked anyway.

He nodded. "When I got there he was collapsed at his dining room table, not breathing. It looked as if he hadn't breathed in a long time. Underneath him was the article about you, sis, in *Chicago Lives*."

He stopped, his eyes sweeping over the room as if he were reliving that moment of discovery. The unconsciousness of it made Boots realize that he was telling the truth, at least in this instance.

"Sis," he said, "he was gone. I didn't know why. I looked around the apartment for drugs, didn't find any. He hadn't cut himself. I almost called 911, but then I realized they would have gotten the wrong idea about the apartment. Lenny wouldn't have wanted that. So after I found his keys I put as much of Lenny as I could into this big duffel bag—you know, sis, that big old hockey bag he bought in L.A.—but even that wasn't big enough. I used the drapes to cover what stuck out. I took the underpass between your two buildings to get to my car."

The image of Lenny doubled up in a duffel bag overwhelmed Penny with grief.

Boots took her hand. "You don't have to go through with this."

"I'm okay," Penny lied. "What next? What else did you do to that poor guy?"

"Sis, he was already dead. I was just trying to make the reality a little less unpleasant for all of us."

Bryson intervened. "Mr. Lane, can we just continue?"

"I left to go to church. I had to preach. It would have been too suspicious had I not gone. I was there around six thirty. At eight or so I left to go to Hyde Park. I had already decided Lenny should die at his real home."

"Mr. Lane," Boots asked, "why did you deny seeing Penny on Sunday night at Family First?"

Benjamin avoided their glances. "I was scared. I lied. I wasn't sure what to say. That was wrong, sis," he said as he looked at Penny. "That was wrong of me. I'm sorry."

"That isn't the only thing that was wrong, Benji. You set me up in the process," Penny stated. "Was that a way to make the reality a little less unpleasant?"

"That wasn't intentional. I was just recreating the scene at his other place. He was already wearing your jacket. He had been all day. The article was there in front of him. Truthfully, sis, that was probably the last thing he saw before he died—"

"Why the gun?" Boots asked.

"It was at Lenny's place." Benjamin shrugged. "I didn't know he had a gun. It was just sitting there on the table, just as if he wanted to end it that way but couldn't get himself to do it. I decided to do it for him. It just seemed like a more manly exit."

And a way to obscure the truth, Boots silently concluded. "Was it an exit you could exploit somehow?" she asked aloud.

Jimmy shot her a warning look, which she interpreted as *This is what got us in trouble last time. Don't push it.*

But Bryson was intrigued and stopped Jimmy's look with a wave. "Mr. Lane, I'm going to ask you if you would answer this. It may or may not be relevant, but we need to pursue all lines of questioning."

Benjamin found his tongue. "I have no idea what you're talking about."

Boots raised her eyebrows in question to Bryson. He waved her on. "Gary Davis told me about one of your heroes, the religious rock performer Gareth Grace. I did a little research on Mr. Grace. Apparently after his death they took his memorial service—a multimedia concert of Grace—on the road. I'd imagine it was much like the service at Family First. You weren't planning on doing something like that, were you?"

Benjamin turned red.

Boots continued. "Mr. Lane, did you love Mr. Blue?"

Jimmy rolled his eyes. Bryson kicked him under the table.

"No, not in that way," Benjamin said, assuming that she meant sexually. "As a brother."

"And have you thought about how you treated him?" Boots asked.

Benjamin sat up straight. "I see nothing wrong with what I did. I was just protecting the integrity of a fellow brother in Christ. I didn't want the press to take his death out of context."

"Benjamin, what the hell are you talking about? What 'context'?" Penny hissed.

"Sis," he said, "don't you get it?"

She and Boots conferred with silent looks; then Bryson said, "I don't think any of us understand what you're driving at, Mr. Lane."

Benjamin Lane's eyes gleamed with tears. "When Lenny visited me on Sunday, he was worried. He was worried that he hadn't been able to love you enough, sis, and that was what drove you to the arms of another man."

"That's ridiculous," Penny said.

Benjamin plowed on. "He could feel all his months of prayer and discipleship going down the drain. He was afraid of reverting to his sinful lifestyle."

The longer he talked, the more Boots got disturbed. "Mr. Lane, did you at any time anticipate Lenny's death? Did he tell you that he was going to do something to himself?"

"No, no," he said, "he wouldn't have done that. Lenny was too smart for that. He knew I would have been forced to stop him."

"Ben," Penny said, "what do you mean, 'forced to stop him'? You do know that it would be better had Lenny lived, don't you?"

Benjamin didn't answer.

Boots slowly understood what he was saying. "'And I say unto you, my friends,'" she quoted, "'be not afraid of them that kill the body, and after that have no more that they can do. But I will forewarn you whom ye shall fear: Fear him who, after he hath killed, hath power to cast into hell; yea, I say unto you, Fear him.' Luke 12:4-5." Boots's detached recital belied her visceral response to these verses taken out of context.

He looked up at Boots with awe. "Precisely, Officer. Lenny knew that the body was the expendable part. The soul is the important part. Lenny is in a much better place now. His soul is safe. No more worry of hellfire. No more struggles. Safe in the arms of Jesus."

Benjamin truly believed Lenny was better dead than queer.

His words sucked the oxygen right out of the room.

Penny stood and stumbled to the door of the room. Unaware the door had been locked behind her, she fumbled with the doorknob.

Benjamin reached his hands out toward Penny. "Sis, you've got to believe me. He would have wanted it this way."

Penny turned around and slapped her brother in the face. No one stopped her. Pulling her eyes away, she frantically knocked on the door. The door was opened and an arm guided Penny through. The door slammed shut.

Boots looked at Benjamin Lane, weighing her words. Standing, she shook her head and headed for the door. She knew that reasoning with this guy was pointless. She knew she shouldn't even bother.

Five seconds later, after she remembered that she was no longer a cop, that she could speak her mind without endangering her job or the case, she changed her mind.

"Mr. Lane," Boots said, "I don't know your God. But I don't believe in a God who would ask a young man in the prime of his life to kill himself because he loved men instead of women. And then to be rewarded by resting in the very manly arms of Jesus in the next life—" Her voice cracked. "This has been an unfortunate and sad case all around. But I think the saddest part in this whole mess is you, Mr. Lane."

She knocked on the door and gained exit from one of the guards.

* * * * * * * * * *

Benjamin was released but was warned that he might want to consult a lawyer about the precarious situation he found himself in. In the cab, his last conversation with Lenny rolled through his memory.

"Ben, I can't be in the band anymore. I can't live a lie anymore. I tried. I gave every ounce of strength I could to fight it."

"Did you really, Len? Did you reach down deep and find that last bit? I don't think you did. Tell me that making love with my sister didn't unleash something deep down, something good, something natural."

"I don't even know how to answer that. It didn't straighten me out, Ben."

"Either way, you don't have to leave the band. Let's look at your options. Of course, you can't marry sis because she's, well, her judgment is all fouled up. You could be celibate."

"So you are telling me that I cannot ever hope to be with another person unless it is a woman. And if I can't be with a woman, then I am destined to be alone."

"Len, not having sex is not the end of the world."

"It's not just about fucking. You know it's deeper than that."

"Like your relationship with Gary was? How deep was that? You've told me about what happened between the two of you. You can't convince me that you shared the love of all time. Len? Len, are you listening to me? Len! Come back here! We haven't even talked about the Chicago Lives *story. We need to stick together. We don't have anyone else."*

I don't have anyone else, thought Benjamin as he looked out the window of the taxi. *Why did you leave me here alone?*

Forty

Penny, Marc, Gary, and Daniel sat in Marc's apartment late Thursday evening. The mood was particularly heavy. They had just pieced enough of the details together to understand the events. No one understood why, however. Benjamin Lane was a very sick person.

Daniel was ready for more uplifting conversation. "Can you believe that it's only been a week?" he said. "You know, since the two of you met?"

And Gary and me, he added silently. Even though Gary was clearly a foot away from Daniel on the couch, he could feel his energy. It was the closest they had been since his visit to Daniel's office on Tuesday. They still hadn't told Penny. Daniel wasn't sure how they were going to without hurting her feelings.

"A week tomorrow, though it seems like longer," Marc commented. "I'm sorry that Boots couldn't be here," he added, referring to this informal debriefing among friends.

"And she will inevitably be at the station for quite a while," Daniel said. "Though I'd bet she doesn't miss the paperwork part of being a cop."

Gary stretched out. "There are some pieces still missing for me. Though I bet Penny or Mr. Weaver here can enlighten us."

"Go for it," Penny said, motioning to Daniel.

"Penny, are you sure you want to hear this again?" After his trial adjourned for the evening, Daniel had hurried to the police station. He had waited for her outside the interrogation room and caught her as she stumbled through the door.

"Penny," Gary said, "I'm sorry. You've been through hell. We don't need to talk about this."

Penny looked deep in her thoughts. "It's not like I'm not already thinking about it. I'm okay. Go ahead."

Daniel started, "I talked with Boots, but there are still holes. As you know, Benjamin was amazingly cooperative, especially after the police found the journals. Unbeknownst to him, Lenny had kept a detailed account of his 'reparative therapy,' as he called it, so we know exactly what Lenny tried to do to become heterosexual. And they are sure Benjamin did not give Lenny the overdose. Apparently he found him when it was too late to do anything about it."

Marc asked, "Then why the faked suicide?"

Daniel sighed. "Ben thought that he was doing Lenny a favor by manipulating the events to point toward the broken engagement. Then," he added, "Lenny would look straight. And Ben didn't want the police to discover the body in Lenny's secret apartment, so he put Lenny into the trunk of his car before the church service. He skipped out right after his sermon. I guess the gun was a dramatic touch. Boots assumes Benjamin read too many Sam Spade books."

Gary said, "What a favor. He set up Penny."

"Benjamin said he didn't mean to do that. For some reason, Lenny had been wearing that coat. Benjamin took it off after, well …" He let the thought trail off. "And he wasn't very smart about it, which in a perverse way adds to the believability of it all. He hid the jacket and the drapes in the Dumpster, not considering that someone would link the two things to Lenny's death. And of course, it was seeing the backdrop in the video that helped Penny place the location of Lenny's video. And the place of death."

Penny looked ahead, glazed. "Lenny did initiate his own death. But the point is moot. Lenny had a hidden condition and had been on and off his medication for months. I believe those things helped push him to the edge. The broken engagement was probably the final straw. But Benny believes that Lenny's death was ultimately a good thing. He told me that, in death, Lenny was better off." She looked pale as she relived the memory of her brother's words.

"That part doesn't make any sense to me," Daniel said. "I thought suicides were supposedly damned to hell. Why would Benjamin think suicide was better than homosexuality?"

"Well," Gary said, "if suicide is somehow a sin, homosexuality is even a greater sin. For a lot of folks, it's the greatest sin. So it's a lesser-of-two-evils kind of thing, I guess."

"Well, suicide is certainly one option taken by plenty of gays and lesbians, especially kids," Marc said. "Though I doubt Leviticus Incorporated would condone such behavior, their 'reparative therapy' certainly sets folks up for failure. You would think that combining the high percentage of suicide among gay youth with the small percentage of people who supposedly change should send that organization a message about the dangers of intolerance."

"I hear you," Daniel said. "I was glad to know that Lenny had participated in Blue Vista's youth group, but it's sad to know he was undone by the same forces that he tried to help kids avoid."

"No one is completely free of that kind of negativity or self-destruction," Marc said. Marc seemed particularly weighted down by all of the events. His own private battle with the Local School Board was taking its toll on him.

"By the way, Marc," Daniel said, "I was talking with one of the partners at my firm. She's willing to take your case if you're interested. And I think that she has some good strategies, including support from the AASF. She's also thinking that maybe a class action suit against *Chicago Lives* may be a good corrective for their lack of journalistic integrity. I'm just grateful they never fingered you. Though with Penny being cleared, the story may fade away, and with it the LSB's decision."

Marc promptly changed the subject. "What about the video?"

Daniel replied, "That video is still one of the strangest parts of this whole damn thing. Boots was glad she had cut it during the memorial service but won't say any more about it. And even though Benjamin had been compiling footage for a video, he claims to have no prior knowledge about that tape. And they're not sure how Penny's jacket got involved."

"I think I've figured out the part about my jacket," Penny said. "On Saturday night, after Lenny caught me with Marc, I could almost swear that he was carrying something. On Sunday afternoon, when I first noticed it gone, I assumed that I had left it here at Marc's. But it wasn't here." She tensed. "Maybe he was sending me a message after all."

"Now that you say that, I remember him picking up a duffel bag." Marc added, "But remember, Pen. He was drunk. He took your jacket, but probably because he knew you liked it a lot. An empty gesture."

Penny sighed. "Maybe you're right."

Marc said, "But one of the first things we'll do after we pack your place up is to go shopping for a new Scarlett O'Hara coat for you."

Penny was caught off guard. "Oh yeah. Right."

"You are moving, then," Daniel said. "Good decision. Find something that will be home to you."

Penny looked enigmatically at Marc. Marc shifted in his seat next to Penny. "I think Pen's working out the details on that one."

Now what's going on? Daniel wondered, picking up the clue that something was wrong between them. The conversation fell into a lull. "Well, I think that's all I can deal with tonight. I should get going."

"Yeah, me too," said Gary. "Blondie, can I catch a ride with you?"

Blondie, Daniel noted with a crooked smile. "Uh, sure, Gary."

They almost got to the door before they heard a voice behind them. "Daniel? Gary?" She looked between the two of them. "There's something going on between the two of you, isn't there?"

They turned around, looking as guilty as two kids caught smoking corn silk behind the barn. "Well—" Daniel started.

Gary was less hesitant. "We wanted to tell you earlier. Penny, remember how I said I met someone at the Blue Vista Ball? Well, it was Blondie here."

Daniel finally found his tongue. "After I figured out who Gary was, he and I agreed to put this—us—on hold until we had gotten you out of hot water."

"Now I understand that little speech you gave me, Dan. About trusting you, blah, blah, blah. And Marc, I bet you knew." Her voice was strangely accusatory.

"Uh, well," he mumbled.

Penny looked pissed. "Dan, you said that I wouldn't be the last to know!"

Gary took Penny in his arms; she resisted at first but finally relaxed. "Sweetheart, you knew before *Chicago Lives*. That's saying quite a bit, especially after this week, isn't it?"

Forty-one

Spooner was getting high on the attention. Damn. Maybe she should close the bar more often. Nothing like sympathy to get the hormones going.

The doctor had let Spooner out of the hospital on Thursday—the same day the police cleared Penny of Lenny Blue's death. Boots divided her attention between Spooner's homecoming and busting the ex-queer brother of Penny's. Having such a full dance card seemed to both annoy and please the lady PI all at once.

"Shit," Spooner had said to Boots in the hospital, "I'm not an invalid. Just dump me off at my place and move on. We'll settle later tonight."

Boots shot her a fierce look that communicated protection. "Don't you dare go to the bar tonight," she ordered.

"Whatcha gonna do, handcuff me to the bed?" Spooner dared.

Boots didn't respond at first. She wheeled Spooner out the door and helped her into her car. Then Boots whispered in Spooner's ear, "I couldn't chain a tiger like you anywhere. Not that I won't try." Boots got into the driver's seat as if there were nothing between them.

Boots was like that. She used the slow-cooker approach to seduction. She knew that her line would slowly burn away in Spooner's brain and leave an insatiable ache for her by tonight.

Spooner hoped she was torturing Boots the same way.

After they were out of the hospital, Boots led Spooner upstairs to her apartment (slowly), then assisted her in undressing (slowly). Just as Spooner was ready to tear into her, Boots found a particularly sensitive place on Spooner's neck and left an imprint of her luscious lips there for everyone in God's creation to see. Then she left.

Spooner redressed (quickly), walked down the stairs (quickly), and headed for the bar.

Even though Spooner enjoyed the attention of the clientele, she appreciated it only as a distraction from her time later with Boots. Was this what it meant to be a bottom? Spooner wondered. She had never allowed herself to be courted before. Spooner hated to admit it, but she was enjoying the ride.

* * * * * * * * * *

Jimmy was eating a hot dog and fries when Boots entered their coffee shop.

"Is the coast clear?" she asked, wondering about their friend Clayvey/Klinger.

"He's back in the slammer," he said. Jimmy loved stereotypical cop words like "slammer" and "joint." "Believe it or not, he was arrested during a non–*M*A*S*H** episode. Clayvey, not Klinger, picked a fight with a guy at his job."

"You're a better detective than I give you credit for," Boots said as she ordered coffee.

"Detective, my foot," Alison, the waitress at the coffee shop, said. "I told him about Clayvey."

Jimmy shrugged. "Doesn't mean I'm not a good detective."

He waited until Alison was busy behind the counter, then filled Boots in on the rest of the details. "The reason we didn't find the victim's car was that he had parked it in an immediate-tow zone near Benjamin Lane's place. The tow truck took it to a Clark Street lot on Sunday afternoon. That's probably the reason Lenny took a cab back to his apartment. The car was clean, except for a few parking tickets. No one thought to look up Leonard Rantzhoff as the owner of the car."

"So Benjamin Lane really didn't know about the car," Boots said.

"He probably didn't know about the videotape either." He dangled the information in front of her like a carrot, waiting for Boots to bite.

She did. "Spill it."

Jimmy did, with almost as much relish as was loaded on his hot dog. "After that drama in the interrogation room, I got a call from a Julio Merchiano, who claimed to have been with Lenny Blue Saturday afternoon and Sunday morning."

Boots wondered why that name sounded familiar. "Was this Merchiano a friend of Blue's?"

"A new friend, if you catch my drift. A new, intimate friend."

Oh.

Jimmy continued. "He remembers Blue wearing a red fringe jacket. Anyway, after they get off on each other for the second time in twenty-four hours—"

Boots rolled her eyes at his unnecessary embellishment.

"—Blue leaves. Then a few minutes later Merchiano gets a call from the security guard that he had a package. Apparently Blue left the videotape with the guard on his way out the door. A note with it instructs Merchiano to have the tape delivered for viewing at his memorial service."

"But he wasn't even dead yet!" Boots said.

Jimmy nodded. "Merchiano freaked. He had only known Blue's first name, and they had done the deed at his apartment, so he didn't have Blue's address. It's not like he could call 911 and report that a man named Lenny was planning to commit suicide. He even watched the video to see if he could find any clues, but without knowing who Blue was, the tape is useless." Jimmy continued with his late dinner.

"So the poor guy had to wait until he read about this guy's death in the paper."

"He didn't have to wait that long. He found out watching the news Sunday night. On Tuesday he found out about the service at Family First, so that's where Merchiano dropped it off. Since Benjamin Lane had already compiled video footage of Blue, the video staff just added the new tape to the pile. Benjamin Lane had absolutely nothing to do with it.

"Merchiano had no idea who Blue was when he got the video. After he found out, he was afraid to reveal anything because he didn't want to be part of a possible homicide case." Jimmy slid a fry into his mouth as he finished the sentence.

"Then why did he come forward now? That was a pretty risky thing."

Jimmy shrugged. "Guilt maybe? Who knows the human mind?"

"Tell me a little more about this Merchiano guy," Boots said.

"He says he's a lawyer in a firm downtown."

"What do you mean, 'says'? Is he or isn't he?"

"There is no Julio Merchiano practicing law in Chicago. It's yet another alias," Jimmy replied. "This has been one goofy-ass case."

Julio Merchiano. The name was ringing multiple bells in Boots's head, but at first she didn't recognize the tune. Then she figured it out. Obviously the cops didn't scratch the surface too deeply. Julio Merchiano was Jules Merchant, a friend of Daniel's and a partner at his firm. She had seen Daniel sitting with Jules and his partner, Pete Winslow, at the Blue Vista Ball. And Jules was probably less afraid of outing himself than outing his affair with another man. Especially if he knew Daniel was involved with the case. Yet his alias was a little too close to Jules's name. Boots wondered if Jules really wanted to be busted. Maybe by Daniel.

"Did Merchiano say he lived by himself? No, uh, roommates?"

"Yes. One, but he left to visit his family Saturday morning. He wasn't due back for two weeks, so he was gone during the whole—" Jimmy squinted at her. "I don't like that look in your eyes. You know who this guy is, don't you?"

Boots put a five on the table and got up. "You're right, Jimmy. This has been one goofy-ass case. But it's a goofy-ass case that's officially closed."

Forty-two

"You know we just left something back there," Daniel said as they pulled out of the parking space.

"Yeah," Gary replied. "I don't have good feelings about it. In the time I've known Penny, I've never seen her so—shaken."

"I've only known her a week and I'd have to agree with you. The look on her face when she came out of that interrogation room, well, I haven't seen that amount of pain in a long time. And I see a lot of pain in my line of work."

Gary looked at Daniel. "How strong is your friend Marc?"

Daniel understood the unspoken question. "He's been through a lot. But everyone has a breaking point." And Marc was dangerously close to the surface at this moment, he feared. They drove in silence for a few minutes. Changing the subject, Daniel said, "I would have liked to meet Lenny."

"You almost did," Gary said.

"What? When?"

"At the benefit. Remember the guy who grabbed me just before we connected? That was him."

"Wow," Daniel said. "I should have remembered that."

They followed a southbound train for about a block; it raced ahead of them as they paused for a stoplight. Gary continued. "He never told me anything, Dan. And yet I never questioned how he knew stuff. The clubs, the people. He had connections, but I never put it together. He found me at the benefit last week, for God's sake. And then at the end he was different. He was not the same guy. I should have figured it out."

Daniel looked at Gary. "How would you have known? It sounds like Lenny kept a lot of stuff to himself. And how could you know that Benjamin was working him over like that? I hope you're not blaming yourself."

"I know all that, but still." A knot of grief threatened to break to the surface, but Gary pushed it back down.

It was taking too long for them to get to Daniel's apartment. "Where are we going?" Gary asked.

"Just driving," Daniel said. "I don't feel like going home right now. Do you?"

"No." Gary watched the train slip away on its tracks. "I'm glad that I met you, Dan. You're the one good thing that came out of this whole shitty mess."

"You too, Cowboy." Daniel's voice was soft. After a long pause he added, "My lover left me last Christmas. I was feeling pretty low when I spotted you across the ballroom. My friends, the ones at the table last Friday night, had just been telling me I needed to move on. You know, they were right. And I'm glad I did. Otherwise I wouldn't have met you."

Gary was silent.

"Maybe you need to be sad for a bit, so you can move on too," Daniel added, understanding Gary all too well. "Go ahead. You can grieve an ex-lover's death. I'm not going to take it personally."

A sob escaped Gary's lips before he could stop it. Daniel pulled over the car and held him. About an hour later Daniel woke up. Gary was still in Daniel's arms, but still very much awake. "Blondie, there is one more thing I need to tell you about me and Lenny."

Forty-three

Daniel and Gary had barely gotten out the door when Penny told Marc that she was going. "You mean, for a walk?" Marc asked. "That's not what you mean, is it?"

Penny sank onto Marc's couch. "I don't know. I need to spend some time alone, to sort this all out."

"What about us? And all that happened this week?"

"That's why I'm going away for a while. I need to figure out who I am and clean up the mess I've created, understand what happened this last week. I can't ruin what we've had."

Had? Marc sank on his knees by Penny. "This doesn't make any sense. We've already come through so much together. Unless ..." He paused. "It's the black thing, isn't it? Or is it because I have a queer sister? You're freaking out because you're finally understanding what the big picture is all about."

"Marc, my life has completely dissolved. One week ago, I knew exactly who I was—"

"Or thought you knew," Marc interjected.

"Maybe. But now I am so confused. Okay, maybe I wasn't what I thought I was, but my God, Marc, everything's changed. Do you know what that feels like?" Then she realized that she was speaking to someone who was suffering loss as well. "I'm sorry. I'm not even being sensitive to what you've gone through this week." She held back her tears. "This is precisely what I mean. I need to be alone for a while."

Marc rose from the floor and walked to the window to watch a train barreling down the tracks toward him and just as quickly, away from him. He thought he knew what it would feel like to be standing in front of that train. "Tonight?" he asked, meaning, When will you leave?

"Tonight," she replied. Silence roared through the room. "Marc, I'm sorry."

"Spooner was right. I don't even have to be gay to experience the cliché of a good lesbian psychodrama."

Penny sat, wishing that she could say the right thing, but after more heavy minutes of silence, she picked up her purse and left.

Marc never turned around, but listened to every step as she left the apartment. Ten seconds of silence; then he watched and listened to Penny walk down the sidewalk away from the apartment.

Forty-four

Daniel was suddenly wide awake. Wishing that he could just say, "Forget it, I don't need to know this little secret," he didn't speak right away. Finally he relented: "Go ahead."

"I lied about something to you and to Penny. Lenny and I didn't completely break it off after the engagement."

Daniel wasn't surprised. "Are you still in love with him?" It was a question he had already asked him.

Gary shook his head, then nodded. "No. Yes. I don't know. I was so incredibly captivated by him. He was truly an amazing person, someone whom I was so deeply connected to, until—" He stared out the window for a full minute.

"Until he stopped treating himself, probably," Daniel said gently. "So what did you do when you knew you were going to lose him to Penny?"

"I still slept with him, but on his terms. Knowing that after sex, he would run to Ben and confess his 'sin.' He said he left my name out of his confessions, but I think Ben knew anyway. Our sex was mostly just that—sex. Actually, it was less than sex. It was so desperate. I'm not sure what was worse, knowing that Lenny just slept with me because he thought he had a 'homosexual demon,' or him discussing it with Ben." He continued to stare out the window. "How I ever allowed that to go on is beyond me. I guess I tried to keep him any way I could.

"The last time was different, though. We had a gig in Madison, but we had a free evening. We all went our separate ways, except for Len and Penny. They went on a date. Only they didn't know that I was watching them, hoping—hell, I don't know what I was hoping. Maybe that she'd call his bluff and end the engagement, or that he would realize that it was wrong to string her along. But they ended up in Penny's room. Realizing they had finally consummated something, I knew that I had finally lost him.

"But then Lenny came to my room. We made love that night. It was beautiful and painful at the same time because we both knew it would be our last time. I told him that after the concert tour was over I would be leaving the band and moving on so that neither of us would continue to live in this hell. Because that night I finally understood his pain. I realized we shared that hell."

Daniel pulled Gary closer. "Penny didn't know about you leaving, did she?"

He shook his head. "No point now. The Chukkas are dead. That's why I was at Ben's on Monday. I told him that when Lenny died, the Chukkas died with him." His voice broke.

Ah, thought Daniel, relieved that he could put one more suspicion to rest. "But there's still something you're not telling me, isn't there, Cowboy?"

Gary nodded. "Lenny beat me at my own game."

Daniel looked him in the eye. "What do you mean?"

Gary shifted his glance. "I was the one who bought the gun, Dan. I was planning to use it Friday night. It was our last concert, and I would permanently end my contract. In effect, I would go away. But when I went to look for it, it was gone. I had assumed that Lenny understood what I had planned to do and tossed it in the Chicago River, but instead he must have taken it home. Benjamin must have found it at Lenny's place and used it on him."

Just when he thought the pieces were fitting together, Daniel realized that they had all been blown apart again. "You mean you were going to kill yourself?"

Gary nodded and looked into Daniel's eyes. "You understand that too well, don't you?" he said, wiping the tears from Daniel's face.

Daniel nodded. "Too well." He tried to stop shaking but found it impossible. "But you have to carry on, don't you?"

Gary understood Daniel's real question: You're going to hang on, right, Cowboy?

It was Gary's turn to hold Daniel. "Don't worry, Blondie. I'm not going anywhere any time soon. I think I've found a reason to hang on."

Daniel nodded. "Good thing." He rubbed the few tears away that had escaped. "But tell me this. What the hell is a Chukka?"

Forty-five

Penny rounded the corner, barely seeing through her tears, and bumped into Boots.

"Ms. Lane, where are you going?"

"I'm not sure," she replied. "I just need to get away and think."

"And what are you getting away from? Is this about what your asshole of a brother said back there? If it is, you are making one gigantic mistake."

For the first time, Boots saw Penny get mad. "I can't even say the phrase 'interracial relationship' without an inner debate. How can I love Marc and not be a hypocrite?"

"Oh, that old thing," Boots chuckled. "Welcome to the world of internalized racism. It's actually quite like internalized homophobia—some of us get double helpings of this shit." Boots smiled. "It's awful at first, but once you learn its tricks, it'll settle down. Penny, no one expects you to be a poster child for enlightenment. Well, at least not yet. You do know your brother is an asshole, don't you?"

"Oh, that I do. But it doesn't take the sting away."

Boots shrugged. "No, it may not. But love is a pretty powerful antidote to that kind of poison." She looked toward Spooner's

Bar and tried not to smile. She was unsuccessful. "You can move forward, hoping for the best, or walk away. I hope for Hawthorne's sake that you choose wisely. If that means that you two end up together, that's great. If it doesn't …" She trailed her thought in a shrug. "No one can make that decision for you. If you'll excuse me, I have an appointment I need to keep."

* * * * * * * * * *

Spooner sensed Boots before she actually came through the door; the love bite she had given Spooner pulsed with anticipation seconds before she swept through the door.

Boots's long hair blew like silk as the wind carried her into the bar. She had changed clothes since Spooner last saw her. She wore a long teal-blue jacket over a simple white shirt; black jeans and her namesake footwear completed the ensemble.

"Well, doll," Spooner said as Boots slid up to the counter, "you look good enough to eat."

"That was the idea," Boots replied. "Now, what was that little thing about handcuffs?"

Epilogue

It was after 4:00 AM and Marc still couldn't sleep. In an attempt to distract himself, he decided on an old reliable method to lull himself to sleep: to work on bills. The mundane nature of the chore helped occupy his spinning thoughts, and he realized that for the first time since Penny left (was it only a few hours ago?), he had successfully moved from heartache to numbness. He was glad.

His electric bill was missing from the stack. He hadn't remembered seeing it. Unlatching the door so as not to lock himself out, Marc walked down the stairs to his mailbox. Because the events of the week had distracted him, he discovered most of one week's worth of mail was crammed in the little box. He struggled to pull it out. The envelopes finally dislodged themselves and exploded all over the entryway of the building. Cursing, he gathered the letters. As he collected the mail, he noticed a package in the corner with a mailing label from Hancock Academy. Someone from the school had delivered it without help from the U.S. Postal Service. Probably some personal item he had left behind. Underneath was an envelope from Andersonville Hospital, addressed to Penny Lane. Resisting the urge to pitch both items out the door, Marc balanced them on top of the other mail and climbed back upstairs.

He dropped the package on the coffee table with the bills and wrote a check to Commonwealth Edison for $77.43. He looked through the rest of the mail, and stopped when he found the bill from Andersonville Hospital. Marc stared at it for a full minute, then opened it. Inside he found an invoice for a twenty-two-dollar box of facial tissues, used during the visit of one Clarrissa Spooner. He didn't know what that was about, was tempted to forward the bill to his clairvoyant sister who always seemed to know best, but instead wrote a check for twenty-two dollars and sealed it in the envelope. He dropped it on the coffee table, then picked it up again and kissed the seal in some type of benediction. Marc suspected the Novocain was wearing off.

To atone for his slip of emotion, or to perhaps distract himself from it, Marc opened every single piece of junk mail. He lingered over his desperate need for another vacuum cleaner, over whether a local service could do his grocery shopping, whether he needed to change cell phone companies, whether he had all the credit he deserved, and whether he should get the platinum card with the lower APR. But eventually the coffee table was cleared of all the mail except for the package.

He stared out the window at the predawn sky. "Oh, fuck it all. Might as well go for high drama," he exhaled as he inserted *Steal Away* into the CD player. He headed toward the kitchen for the obligatory glass of red wine and a knife from the cutlery block, returning just in time for the second verse of "Steal Away," the song he and Penny had chosen at the jukebox a week earlier:

I can see a look in your eyes that sometimes wanders to catch a glimpse, a stare.

It was that look that first caught me in a web of desire; I thought you loved, cared.

The gossamer cord that you've tied to my heart does stretch and break.

And the alchemy binding my life yours is lead with despair.

There's no more smoke, no mirrors; I couldn't see clearer.
You've left the cage, but stolen my heart away.

Marc began hacking at the strapping tape and finally dislodged the inside contents, which were composed of two notes and something soft wrapped in bright balloon wrapping paper.

The handwriting in both letters was immediately recognizable. The first letter was from Shannon Doyle:

Marc,

Your student, Fiona Clarke, wanted you to have this. Since her stepfather said she was quite distraught about you leaving, I thought it might make her feel better knowing that you got this.

Frankly, it'll be a hell of a long time until I feel better about this whole thing.

S.

The second was from Fiona Clarke:

Dear Dr. H,

It's about that note I left for you in the classroom. I was hoping that I was wrong for once, but I know that you're not going to teach at Hancock anymore. I found out because Jesse Gordon is here at Disney World too, and I saw him when he was getting his picture taken with Goofy and he said he heard you were leaving. I guess he would know since his mother is the lunch lady and all. When I found out, I made Tony (the H., you know what I mean) take me to one of those mailing stores and I sent you this package. Actually, I had to send it to the school since I didn't have your address, but I made him send it fast so that you would get it quick. The paper is kinda stupid since they only had baby paper or ugly-looking flowers, so I got you the balloons because they're cheery, I hope. I had another feeling about you, that the woman I talked about in my last note was going to hurt you, but then I also knew that everything would work out okay and you'd be happy. But it would be sorta messy as well. But since you work with kids, I think you are okay with messy stuff. And this is a sweater that you may remember me wearing. My mother said it's too tight for me and threw it in the garbage. I pulled it out because I think it would fit you since you won't grow any bigger. Or maybe it'll fit the woman. That's okay too. And when you have a little girl she can wear it when she's in the fourth grade unless she's bigger like me.

Fiona

PS I'm sorry the last note was a mess.

Marc's tears ran during the last part of the message, but even though the words were blurred he got the idea. He carefully opened the balloon paper and pulled out the sweater he had last seen Fiona wear: a brown rag-wool pullover. He slipped off his shirt and put the sweater on. It was snug but comforting. And, though he had steeled himself from the pain of loss, he now wept with the conflicting feelings of sadness and a childlike glimmer of hope.

It was in the midst of the tears that Marc realized that another voice had joined the CD, changing the words slightly from the recording:

Can it ever be like it was that night when your smile opened my heart?

Can I ever return; can I ever return, can I return, my love?

And how can you trust me again (and again and again and again)?

Unless I open the door—unless I open my heart

Unless I open the wound—unless I open the pain
I will never, never know.

And let you steal
Let you steal
Steal my heart
Away.

Penny stood in the doorway, eyes bright with tears, as the song ended on the stereo.

"Well," she said. "Can I come in?"

"Only if it's for good," Marc answered, his voice wavering.

"Are you sure that's what you want? I've been nothing but trouble."

Marc pulled her over the threshold and into his arms. "Oh, Pen, I don't think I'd be satisfied with anything less at this point. But first answer me this. Do you love me?" he whispered.

The tears dropped from Penny's lashes. "I do love you. I was a fool to walk out just then."

"Shhh," Marc said, wiping the tears from Penny's cheeks. "Just this, just us, just now. No other questions. No more explanations. Clean slate."

Penny nodded.

Marc took his lover's hand and led her into the bedroom.

About the Author

Veronica Neill grew up in a small rural community in Wisconsin. She earned a bachelor's degree in English and communications and completed graduate work in theology and education. Neill has a deep interest in spirituality and helped create an interfaith spirituality center for gay, lesbian, bisexual and transgendered people and their friends in Chicago. She lives in northeast Illinois.